948

$6.00
11.00

Alessandro Baricco

THE YOUNG BRIDE

*Translated from the Italian
by Ann Goldstein*

Europa
editions

Europa Editions
214 West 29th Street
New York, N.Y. 10001
www.europaeditions.com
info@europaeditions.com

Translation by Ann Goldstein
Original title: *La Sposa giovane*
Translation copyright © 2016 by Europa Editions

Library of Congress Cataloging in Publication Data is available
ISBN 978-1-60945-334-3

Baricco, Alessandro
The Young Bride

Book design by Emanuele Ragnisco
www.mekkanografici.com

Cover illustration by Tanino Liberatore

Prepress by Grafica Punto Print – Rome

Printed in the USA

To Samuele, Sebastiano, and Barbara. Thank you.

There are thirty-six stone steps to climb, and the old man climbs slowly, cautiously, almost as if he were collecting them, one by one, to drive them up to the second floor: he the shepherd, they meek animals. Modesto is his name. He has served in this house for fifty-nine years, and is therefore its priest.

Reaching the top step he stops before the wide hall that stretches without surprises before his gaze: to the right are the closed rooms of the Masters, five; to the left seven windows, dimmed by shutters of lacquered wood.

It's just dawn.

The old man stops because he has a tally to update. He records the mornings that he has inaugurated in this house, always in the same way. So he adds a number that vanishes into the thousands. The count is dizzying, but he isn't disturbed by it: officiating forever at the same morning rite seems to him consistent with his job, respectful of his inclinations, and typical of his fate.

After running the palms of his hands over the ironed fabric of his pants—along the sides, at the thigh—he moves his head forward slightly and sets his feet in motion again. He ignores the doors of the Masters, but, reaching the first window, on the left, he stops to open the shutters. He does this with fluid and precise gestures. He repeats them at every window, seven times. Only then does he turn, to assess the shafts of dawn light entering through the glass: he knows its every possible nuance and from its character can tell what sort of day it will be; he can deduce from it, sometimes, faded promises. Since they will rely on him—all of them—the judgment he forms is important.

Hazy sun, light breeze, he decides. So it will be.

Then he goes back along the corridor, this time devoting himself to the side he ignored before. He opens the doors of the Masters, one after another, and announces the start of the day with a phrase that he repeats aloud five times, altering neither timbre nor inflection.

Good morning. Hazy sun, light breeze.

Then he disappears.

He no longer exists, until he reappears, unchanged, in the breakfasts room.

The tradition of that solemn awakening, which later becomes joyful and drawn out, derives from long-ago events whose details we prefer not to speak of for now. It concerns the entire household. Never before dawn: this is imperative. The Masters wait for the light and for Modesto's dance at the seven windows. Only then do they consider the condemnation to bed, the blindness of sleep, and the risk of dreams to be over. They are dead: the old man's voice returns them to life.

Then they swarm out of the rooms, without putting on clothes, not even pausing for the relief of some water on the eyes, on the hands. With the odors of sleep in hair and teeth, we meet in the halls, on the stairs, in the doorways of the rooms, embracing like exiles returning from some distant land, incredulous at having survived the spell that night seems to us. Dispersed by the obligation to sleep, we re-establish ourselves as a family, and on the ground floor we flow into the big breakfasts room like an underground river coming into the light, carrying a premonition of the sea. Most of the time we are laughing.

The table for breakfasts—a term that no one ever thought of using in the singular, for only a plural can conjure the richness, the abundance, and the unreasonable duration—is indeed a well-laid sea. A pagan sense of thanksgiving is evident—the escape from the catastrophe of sleep. Modesto, with two servants, watches over everything, gliding imperceptibly. On a normal day, neither Lent nor a holiday, the ordinary offerings include white and dark toast, curls of butter on a silver plate, honey, chestnut spread, and a jam made with nine fruits, eight varieties of pastry culminating in an inimitable croissant, four different flavors of cake, a bowl of whipped cream, fruit in season always cut with mathematical precision, a display of rare exotic fruits, newly laid eggs cooked three different ways, fresh cheeses plus an English Stilton, thin slices of prosciutto from the farm, cubes of mortadella, beef broth, fruit braised in red wine, cornmeal cookies, anise digestive tablets, marzipan cherries, hazelnut ice cream, a pitcher of hot chocolate, Swiss pralines, licorice, peanuts, milk, coffee.

Tea is detested, chamomile only for the sick.

It's understandable, then, how a meal considered by most people a quick start to the day is in this house a complex and interminable process. The usual practice keeps them at the table for hours, crossing over into the zone of lunch (which in fact in this house no one ever gets around to), as in an Italian imitation of the more stylish "brunch." Only every so often, a few at a time, they get up, to then reappear at the table partly dressed, or washed—bladders emptied. But these details are scarcely noticed. Because, it should be said, the visitors of the day—relatives, acquaintances, postulants, suppliers, possible authorities, men and women of the church—are arriving at the big table: each with his subject to discuss. It's the habit of the Family to receive them there, during the torrential flow of breakfast, with a sort of ostentatious informality that no one, not even they, would be able to distinguish from the height of arrogance, that is, to receive visitors while wearing pajamas. But the freshness of the butter and the mythical perfection of the tarts induce cordiality. The champagne is always on ice, and poured generously, which is itself sufficient motivation for many.

Thus it is not unusual to see dozens of people at the same time around the breakfasts table, although the family itself is just five, or rather four, now that the Son is on the Island.

The Father, the Mother, the Daughter, the Uncle.

The Son temporarily abroad, on the Island.

Finally, around three in the afternoon, they withdraw to their rooms and, half an hour later, emerge splendidly elegant and fresh, as all acknowledge. We devote the middle hours of the afternoon to business—the factory, the farms, the house. At dusk, solitary work—we meditate, invent, pray—or courtesy visits. Dinner is late and frugal, taken without ceremony, eaten in bits and pieces: it dwells under the wing of night, so we tend to hurry it, like a pointless prelude. Then, without saying good night, we go to the uncertainty of sleep, each of us exorcising it in our own way.

For a hundred and thirteen years, it should be said, all of us have died at night, in our family.

That explains everything.

The particular subject, that morning, was the usefulness of sea bathing, about which the Monsignor, shoveling whipped cream into his mouth, harbored some reservations. He sensed an obvious moral unknown, without daring, however, to define it precisely.

The Father, a good-natured and, if necessary, fierce man, was helping him bring the matter into focus.

"Kindly remind me, Monsignor, where, exactly, it's mentioned in the Gospel."

As a counterweight to the response, which was evasive, the front doorbell rang, rousing little attention, since it was obviously yet another visit.

Modesto took care of it. He opened the door and found before him the young Bride.

She wasn't expected that day, or maybe she was, but they had forgotten about it.

I'm the young Bride, I said.

You, Modesto noted. Then he looked around, astonished, because it didn't make sense that I had arrived alone, and yet there was no one, as far as the eye could see.

They left me at the end of the street, I said. I wanted to count my steps in peace. And I placed the suitcase on the ground.

I was eighteen years old, which was what had been agreed on.

I really would have no hesitation about being naked on the beach—the Mother was saying, meanwhile—since I've always had a certain preference for the mountains (many of her syllogisms were in fact inscrutable). I could cite at least ten people, she continued, whom I've seen naked, and I'm not talking about children or old people who were dying, for whom I have a special, deep sympathy, even though . . .

She broke off when the young Bride entered the room, not so much because the young Bride had entered the room but because she was introduced by an alarming cough from Modesto. Maybe I haven't said that in fifty-nine years of service the old man had refined a laryngeal communication system that everyone in the family had learned to decipher as if it were cuneiform. There was no need for the violence of words, for a cough—or, rarely, two, in the most articulated variants—accompanied his gestures like a suffix that clarified their meaning. At table, for example, he did not serve a single dish without adding a qualification from the epiglottis that encapsulated his own very personal judgment. In the specific situation, he introduced the young Bride with a just noticeable, distant hiss. It indicated, everyone knew, a very high level of vigilance, and that is the reason that the Mother broke off, something that she didn't usually do, since announcing a guest, under normal circumstances, was no different from the filling of her glass with water—she would then calmly drink it. She broke off, therefore, turning toward the new arrival. She registered her youth and, with the automatic politeness of her class, said

Darling!

She hadn't the least idea who it was.

Then a chink must have opened in her habitually muddled mind, because she asked

What month is today?

Someone answered May, probably the Pharmacist, whom champagne rendered unusually precise.

Then the Mother repeated Darling!, but conscious, this time, of what she was saying.

It's incredible how quickly May arrived this year, she was thinking.

The young Bride made a slight bow.

They had forgotten, that was all. It was what had been agreed to, but so long ago that a precise memory of it was lost. One mustn't deduce from that that they had changed their mind: it would have been, in any case, too much work. Once a decision was made in that house, it never changed, for obvious reasons of economy of emotions. Simply, the time had passed with a velocity that they hadn't needed to register, and now the young Bride was there, probably to do what had long ago been agreed to, with the official approval of all: marry the Son.

It was annoying to admit that, strictly speaking, the Son wasn't there.

Yet it didn't seem urgent to linger on that detail, and so what they readily offered was a happy chorus of greeting, veined variously with surprise, relief, and gratitude: the last for the way life proceeded, seemingly heedless of human distractions.

Since I've now begun to tell this story (this, in spite of the distressing series of troubles that have hit me, which would have counseled against such an undertaking), I can't avoid clarifying the geometry of the facts, just as I'm remembering it, little by little, noting, for example, that the Son and the young Bride had met when she was fifteen and he eighteen, and had gradually recognized in each other a magnificent corrective to the hesitations of the heart and to the boredom of youth. At the moment it's premature to explain by what singular course, but it's important to know that they quickly reached the happy conclusion that they wanted to get married. To their respective families the thing seemed incomprehensible, for reasons that I will perhaps be able to explain if the vise of this sadness will loosen its grip: but the unusual personality of the Son, which sooner or later I'll have the strength to describe, and the pure determination of the young Bride, which I'd like to find the clearheadedness to communicate, advised a certain prudence. It was agreed that it was better to put up with it, and they moved on to untying some technical knots, first among them the imperfect alignment of their respective social positions. It should be remembered that the young Bride was the only daughter of a rich animal breeder who had five sons, while the Son belonged to a family that for three generations had been reaping profits from the production and sale of wools and fabrics of a particular quality. There was money on both sides: but undoubtedly it was money of different types, one produced by looms and ancient elegance, the other by manure and atavistic hard work. This fact led to an open space of placid indecision that was crossed when, on impulse, the Father communicated solemnly that the marriage between agrarian wealth and industrial finance represented the natural development of the entrepreneurialism of the North, tracing a distinct path of transformation for the entire country. From this he deduced the need to overcome social hierarchies that by now belonged to the past. Given that he formalized the thing in those exact terms, lubricating the sequence with a couple of big, deliberately placed curses, the reasoning seemed convincing to everyone, in its irreproachable mixture of rationality and genuine instinct. We decided to wait just until the young Bride became a little less young: we had to avoid possible comparisons between such a carefully considered marriage and certain peasant unions, hurried and vaguely animallike. Waiting, besides being undoubtedly convenient, seemed to us the seal of a superior moral attitude. The local clergy did not hesitate to confirm, oblivious of the curses.

So they would be married.

Since I'm here, and because tonight I feel a kind of illogical carelessness, brought on, perhaps, by the mournful light in this room they've lent me, I'd like to add something about what happened shortly after the announcement of the engagement, on the initiative, surprisingly, of the young Bride's father. He was a taciturn man, perhaps good in his way, but also irascible, or unpredictable, as if too close proximity to work animals had transmitted a sort of harmless impetuosity. One day he said tersely that he had decided to attempt an ultimate coup in his affairs by emigrating to Argentina, to conquer lands and markets whose every detail he had studied on shitty, fog-bound winter evenings. The people who knew him, vaguely bewildered, decided that such a decision must have something to do with the prolonged coldness of the marriage bed, along with, perhaps, a certain illusion of belated youth, and probably a childish intimation of infinite horizons. He crossed the ocean with three sons, of necessity, and the young Bride, for consolation. He left his wife and the other sons to watch over the land, promising that they would join him, if things went as they should, which in effect he then did, after a year, even selling all his property in his homeland and betting his entire patrimony on the gambling table of the pampas. Before leaving, though, he made a visit to the Father of the Son and affirmed on his honor that the young Bride would appear when she turned eighteen, to fulfill the promise of marriage. The two men shook hands in what was, in those parts, a sacred gesture.

As for the betrothed pair, they said goodbye in apparent tranquility and secret dismay: they had, I must say, good reasons for both.

Once the landowners had set sail, the Father spent some days in a silence unusual for him, neglecting routines and habits that he considered inviolable. Some of his most unforgettable decisions were born of similar personal suspensions, and so the whole Family was resigned to important news when, finally, the Father made a brief but very clear announcement. He said that each of us has his Argentina, and that for them, leaders in the textile sector, Argentina was called England. In fact he had for a while been looking across the Channel at certain factories that were optimizing production in a surprising way: head-spinning profits could be read between the lines. We have to go and see, said the Father, and possibly imitate. Then he turned to the Son.

You'll go, now that you're settled, he said, cheating a little on the terms of the matter.

So the Son had left, even quite happily, on a mission to study the secrets of the English and bring back the best of them, for the future prosperity of the Family. No one expected that he would return within a few weeks, and then no one realized that he wouldn't return even within a few months. But they were like that: they ignored the passing of the days, because they aimed at living only a single, perfect day, infinitely repeated: so time for them was a phenomenon with variable margins that echoed in their lives like a foreign language.

Every morning, from England, the Son sent us a telegram, always with the same text: *All is well*. He was referring, obviously to the trap that was night. At home it was the only news we truly wanted to know: for the rest, it would have been a struggle for us to doubt that during that prolonged absence the Son could do anything but his duty, laced at most with some mild, enviable diversion. Evidently the English factories were numerous and merited close analysis. We stopped expecting him, since he would return.

But the young Bride returned first.

Let us get a look at you, said the Mother, radiant, once the table had reassembled.

They all looked at her.

They picked up a nuance they wouldn't have known how to express.

The Uncle expressed it, waking from a sleep that he had been in for a while, lying in a chair—a champagne glass, full to the brim, in his hand.

You must have done a lot of dancing, signorina, over there. I'm glad of it.

Then he took a sip of champagne and fell asleep again.

The Uncle was a welcome, and irreplaceable, figure in the family. A mysterious syndrome, whose only known sufferer he was, kept him in a constant sleep from which he emerged for very brief intervals, for the sole purpose of participating in the conversation with a precision that we were all now used to considering obvious but that was, clearly, illogical. Something in him was able to register, even in sleep, any event and every word. Indeed, the fact that he came from elsewhere often seemed to give him such lucidity, or such a singular view of things, that his wakings and relevant utterances were endowed with an almost oracular, prophetic resonance. This reassured us greatly, because we knew we could count at any moment on the reserves of a mind so rested that it could completely untangle any knot that appeared in domestic discussion or daily life. In addition, we rather liked the astonishment of strangers encountering those singular feats, a detail that made our house even more attractive. Returning to their families, the guests often took with them the legendary memory of that man who could, while sleeping, be halted even in complex movements, of which holding a champagne glass full to the brim was but a pale example. He could shave in his sleep, and on occasion he had been seen to play the piano as he slept, although he took slightly slowed-down tempos. There were even those who claimed to have seen him play tennis in a deep sleep: it seems that he woke only at the change of sides. I refer to him out of necessity to the story, but also because today I seemed to glimpse a coherence in everything that is happening to me, and so for a few hours it's been easy to hear sounds that otherwise, in the grip of confusion, I would find inaudible: for example, often, the clattering of life on the marble table of time, like dropped pearls. The need of the living to be funny—that in particular.

Ah, yes, you must have danced a lot, the Mother affirmed, I couldn't have said it better, and besides I've never loved fruit pies (many of her syllogisms were in fact inscrutable).

The tango? asked the notary Bertini, agitated. For him, uttering the word "tango" was in itself sexual.

The tango? Argentina? In that climate? asked the Mother, though it wasn't clear whom she was addressing.

I can assure you that the tango is clearly Argentine in origin, the notary insisted.

Then the voice of the young Bride was heard.

I lived in the pampas for three years. Our neighbor was two days away by horseback. A priest brought us the Eucharist once a month. Once a year we'd set out for Buenos Aires, with the idea of attending the première of the Opera Season. But we never arrived in time. It was always much farther than we thought.

Definitely not very practical, the Mother observed. How did your father think he would find you a husband like that?

Someone pointed out to her that the young Bride was engaged to her Son.

It's obvious, you think I didn't know? I made a general observation.

But it's true, the young Bride said, they dance the tango over there. It's lovely, she said.

The mysterious oscillation of space that always heralded the Uncle's imponderable awakenings could be felt.

The tango gives a past to those who don't have one and a future to those who don't hope for one. Then he fell asleep again.

While the Daughter, on the chair next to the Father, watched, silently.

She was the same age as the young Bride—it's many years, incidentally, since I was that age. (Now, thinking back, I see only a great confusion, but also—what seems to me interesting—the waste of an unprecedented and unused beauty. Which, moreover, brings me back to the story that I intend to tell, if only to save my life, but certainly also for the simple reason that telling it is my job.) The Daughter, I was saying. She had inherited from the Mother a beauty that in that region was aristocratic: for the women of that land enjoyed only limited flashes of splendor—the shape of the eyes, two good legs, raven black hair—never that complete and full perfection (apparently the product of improvements made over centuries in the procession of countless generations) which the Mother retained and which she, the Daughter, miraculously replicated, with the gilding, moreover, of youth. And up to there everything was fine. But the truth appears when I emerge from my graceful immobility and move, shifting irreparable amounts of unhappiness, owing to the unalterable fact that I am a cripple. An accident, I was around eight. A cart out of control, a horse shying suddenly on a narrow city street, houses close on either side. Renowned doctors, called from abroad, did the rest—maybe it was bad luck, not even incompetence—but in a complicated, painful way. When I walk I drag one leg, the right, which although perfectly shaped is unreasonably heavy and has no idea how to harmonize with the rest of the body. The foot lands heavily and is partly numb. The arm isn't normal, either; it seems capable of only three positions, none very graceful. You might call it a mechanical arm. Thus, seeing me get up from a chair and come toward you, in greeting, or as a gesture of courtesy, is a strange experience, of which the word disappointment can give a pale idea. Unspeakably beautiful, I disintegrate at the slightest movement, in an instant turning admiration into pity and desire into unease.

It's something I know. But I have no inclination for sadness, or talent for suffering.

While the conversation had moved on to the late flowering of the cherry trees, the young Bride went over to the Daughter and leaned over to kiss her on the cheeks. She didn't get up, because at that moment she wished to be beautiful. They spoke in low voices, as if they were old friends, or perhaps out of the sudden desire to become so. Instinctively, the Daughter understood that the young Bride had learned distance, and would never discard it, having chosen it as her own inimitable form of elegance. She'll always be innocent and mysterious, she thought. They'll adore her.

Then, when the first empty champagne bottles were being carried off, the conversation had an almost magical moment of collective suspension, and in that silence the young Bride asked politely if she could pose a question.

But of course, darling.

Is the Son not here?

The Son? said the Mother, to give the Uncle time to emerge from his elsewhere and help out, but since nothing happened, Ah, the Son, of course, the Son, obviously, my Son, yes, it's a good question. Then she turned to the Father. Dear?

In England, said the Father, with complete serenity. Do you have an idea of what England is, signorina?

I think so.

There. The Son is in England. But temporarily.

In the sense that he'll be back?

Certainly, as soon as we summon him.

And you'll summon him?

It's definitely something we ought to do as soon as possible.

This very day, the Mother specified, unfurling a particular smile that she kept for important occasions.

So that afternoon—and not before he had exhausted the liturgy of breakfast—the Father sat down at his desk and undertook to record what had happened. He did this, usually, with some delay—I refer to the recording of the facts of life, and especially those that involved some disorderliness—but I wouldn't want this to be interpreted as a form of sluggish inefficiency. It was, in reality, a reasonable precaution, on doctor's orders. As everyone knew, the Father was born with what he liked to define as "an imprecision of the heart," an expression that should not be placed in a sentimental context: something irreparable had torn in his cardiac muscle when he was still a hypothesis under construction in his mother's womb, and so he was born with a heart of glass, which first the doctors and later, in consequence, he was resigned to. There was no cure, except for a prudent and slowed-down approach to the world. If you believed the books, a particular shock, or an unprepared-for emotion, would carry him off immediately. The Father, however, knew from experience that this should not be taken too literally. He had understood that he was on loan to life, and he had drawn from that a tendency toward caution, an inclination to order, and the confused certainty of inhabiting a special destiny. To this should be attributed his natural good humor and occasional ferocity. I would like to add that he didn't fear death: he had such familiarity, not to say intimacy, with it that he was absolutely certain he would sense its arrival in time to use it well.

So, that day, he wasn't in a particular hurry to record the appearance of the young Bride. Yet, with the usual tasks taken care of, he didn't avoid the job that awaited him: he bent over his desk and without hesitation composed the text of the telegram, conceiving it with respect for the elementary requirements of economy and the intention of achieving the unequivocal clarity that was necessary. It bore these words:

Young Bride returned. Hurry.

The Mother, for her part, decided that, no question, the young Bride, having no home of her own, and in a certain sense not even a family since every possession and every relative had moved to South America, would stay with them to wait. Since the Monsignor didn't seem to offer any moral objection, despite the Son's absence from the family roof, she asked Modesto to get the guest room ready, which they didn't know much about, since no one ever stayed in it. They were moderately sure that it existed, however. It had the last time.

There's no need for any guest room—she'll sleep with me, the Daughter said tranquilly. She was sitting down, and at those moments her beauty was such that no one could refuse her.

If you'd like to, naturally, the Daughter added, seeking the young Bride's gaze.

I would, said the young Bride.

So she joined the Household, which she had imagined that she would enter as a wife, and now instead found herself sister, daughter, guest, pleasing presence, decoration. Doing so turned out to be natural to her, and she quickly learned the habits and tempos of an unfamiliar way of life. She noted its strangeness, but seldom went so far as to suspect its absurdity. A few days after her arrival, Modesto approached and respectfully let her understand that if she felt the need for any explanations it would be his privilege to enlighten her.

Are there rules that have escaped me? asked the young Bride.

If I may, I will point out just four, so as not to put too many irons in the fire, he said.

All right.

The night is feared, but I imagine you've already been informed of that.

Yes, of course. I thought it was a legend, but I see that it's not.

Exactly. And that is the first.

To fear the night.

To respect it, let's say.

To respect it.

Precisely. Second: unhappiness is not welcome.

Oh, no?

Don't misunderstand me, the thing must be understood in its correct context.

Which is what?

In the course of three generations, the Family has amassed a considerable fortune, and if you happen to wonder how it achieved such a result may I suggest the answer: talent, courage, malice, lucky mistakes, and a profound, consistent, flawless sense of economy. When I speak of economy I don't mean only money. This family wastes nothing. Do you follow me?

Of course.

You see, here they tend to believe that unhappiness is a waste of time and hence a form of luxury that for a number of years yet cannot be allowed. Maybe some tomorrow. But, for now, there is no circumstance of life, however painful, from which souls may be permitted to steal more than a momentary confusion. Unhappiness steals time from joy, and in joy prosperity is built. If you think about it for a moment, it's very simple.

May I raise an objection?

Please.

If they are such maniacs for economy, how does that fit with those breakfasts?

They aren't breakfasts: they are rites of thanksgiving.

Ah.

And then I said a sense of economy, not stinginess, a characteristic completely alien to the Family.

I understand.

I'm sure—these are nuances that you are certainly able to grasp.

Thank you.

There is a third rule to which I would draw your attention, if I may continue to impose on your time.

Take advantage. If it were up to me, I would listen to you for hours.

Do you read books?

Yes.

Don't.

No?

Do you see books in this house?

No, in fact, now that you point it out, no.

Exactly. There are no books.

Why?

The Family has great faith in things, in people, and in themselves. They don't see the need to resort to palliatives.

I'm not sure I understand.

Life already has everything, provided you listen to it, and books are a useless distraction from that task, which this entire family attends to with such dedication that a man engaged in reading, in these rooms, would necessarily seem a deserter.

Surprising.

Debatable, too. But I consider it right to emphasize that this tacit rule is interpreted very strictly in this house. May I make a modest confession?

I would be honored.

I love to read, so I keep a book hidden in my room, and I devote some time to it, before going to sleep. But never more than one. When I finish it, I destroy it. This is not to suggest that you do the same; it's so that you'll understand the gravity of the situation.

I think I understand, yes.

Good.

There was a fourth rule?

Yes, but it's more or less self-evident.

Tell me.

As you know, the Father has an imprecision in his heart.

Of course.

Don't expect from him distractions from a general, necessary tranquility. Or claim them, naturally.

Naturally. Is he really in danger of dying at any moment, as they say?

I'm afraid so, yes. But you must realize that during the daylight hours there is practically no danger.

Ah, yes.

Good. I think that's all, for now. No, one more thing.

Modesto hesitated. He was wondering if it was necessary to proceed with making the young Bride literate, or if it was a useless effort, if not actually imprudent. He remained silent for a moment, then gave two coughs, rather dry and close together.

Do you think you could memorize what you just heard?

The coughs?

They aren't coughs, they are a warning. Kindly consider them my respectful system for alerting you, if necessary, to possible errors.

Let me hear them again . . .

Modesto produced an exact replica of the laryngeal message.

Two dry coughs, close together, I understand. Pay attention.

Exactly.

Are there many others?

More than what I am willing to reveal to you before your marriage, signorina.

All right.

Now I really must go.

You've been very helpful, Modesto.

It was what I hoped to be able to be.

May I repay you in some way?

The old man looked up at her. For an instant he felt he might express one of the childish requests that surfaced in his mind unchecked, but then he remembered that distance was a measure of humility, and of the nobility of his office, so he lowered his gaze and, with an almost imperceptible bow, confined himself to saying that an occasion would surely arise. He left, taking the first steps backward and then turning around as if a gust of wind, and not a disrespectful choice, had decided for him—a technique of which he was a peerless master.

But there were also *different days,* obviously.

Every other Thursday, for example, early in the morning, the Father went to the city: often accompanied by his trusted cardiologist, Dr. Acerbi, he was welcomed at the bank, visited his trusted tradesmen—tailor, barber, dentist, but also suppliers of cigars, shoes, hats, walking sticks, and, occasionally, confessors—had at the proper time a substantial lunch, and finally allowed himself what he usually called an elegant walk. The elegance came from the pace he assumed and the route he chose: the former never careless, the latter along the streets of the center. He almost always ended the day at the brothel, but, keeping in mind the imprecision of his heart, he interpreted the practice as something hygienic, so to speak. Convinced that a certain release of bodily fluids was necessary to the equilibrium of his organism, he had found women available there who were able to provoke it almost painlessly, meaning by pain any excitement that could crack the glass of his heart. Insisting on such prudence from the Mother would have been vain, and, besides, the two slept in separate rooms; although they loved each other deeply, they hadn't chosen each other, as will become clear, for reasons having to do with their bodies. The Father came out of the brothel in the late afternoon. On the way home he reflected: his fierce decisions often had their origins there.

Every month, but on different days, Comandini, the firm's business manager, arrived, announced by a telegram forty-eight hours in advance. Then every custom was sacrificed to the urgency of business, the guests put off, the breakfasts pared to the bone, and the life of the House handed over to the torrential narrations of that little man with nervous gestures who knew, by unfathomable means, what people would want to wear the next year, or how to get them to want the fabrics that the Father had decided to produce the year before. He was rarely mistaken, he could negotiate in seven languages, he squandered everything gambling, and he had a fondness for redheads. Years before, he had emerged unhurt from a frightful train wreck: since then he had stopped eating white meat and playing chess, but had given no explanation.

During Lent the spectacle of the breakfasts was reduced, on holidays everyone wore white, and they skipped the night of the Patron Saint, which fell in June, by gambling. The first Saturday of the month there was music, a gathering of amateurs from the neighborhood and, occasionally, professional singers remunerated with English tweed jackets. On the last day of summer the Uncle organized a bicycle race open to everyone, while at Carnival they had for years hired a Hungarian magician who, with age, had become little more than a good-natured entertainer. At the Immaculate Conception they killed a pig under the guidance of a butcher famous for his stutter, and in November, in years when the fog thickened to an offensive consistency, they organized—often making a sudden decision, dictated by exasperation—a rather solemn ball, at which, with contempt for the milky darkness outside, they burned a number of candles surprising in every respect: it was as if a quivering late-summer-afternoon sun were beating down on the parquet-floored room, unleashing dance steps that returned everyone to a kind of South of the soul.

Normal days, on the other hand, as has been said, adhering to the facts, and speaking concisely—those were all marvelously the same.

The result was a sort of dynamic order that, in the family, was considered flawless.

In the meantime June came in, gliding on English telegrams that put off the Son's return almost invisibly, but after all sensibly, reasonable and precise as they were. In the end, the Great Heat arrived first—oppressive, pitiless, punctual every summer, in that land—and the young Bride felt it, as she struggled to remember it after her Argentine life, recognizing it finally, conclusively, precisely one night, in the damp-filled darkness, while she tossed in her bed, sleepless for once, she who, uniquely in that house, fell asleep as if it were a blessing. She tossed and turned and, with a gesture that surprised her, irritably took off her nightgown, dropping it carelessly, and then lay on her side, bare skin against the linen sheets, to receive the gift of a temporary coolness. I did it spontaneously, because the darkness in the room was thick, and with the Daughter, in her bed a few steps away, I had by now established a sisterly intimacy. Once the light was out we usually talked long enough for some comments, some secrets, then we said goodnight and entered the night, and now, for the first time, I wondered what that sort of faint sonorous song was that rose from the Daughter's bed every night, once the light was out and the secrets and the words had been exhausted, after the usual goodnight—it rose and hovered in the air for a long period whose end I never heard, for I always slipped into sleep, I alone, in that house, without fear. But it wasn't a song—there was a hint of a moan, almost animal—and on that oppressive summer night I wished to understand it because the heat was keeping me awake and my unclothed body made me different. So I let the song hover for a while, to comprehend it better, and then, in the dark, point-blank, I asked calmly, What is it?

The song stopped hovering.

For a moment there was only silence.

Then the Daughter said, You don't know what it is?

No.

Really?

Really.

How is that possible?

The young Bride knew the answer, she knew the exact day when she had chosen that ignorance and could have explained in detail why she had chosen it. But she said simply, I don't know.

She heard the Daughter laugh softly, and then some faint noises, and a match that scraped and flared and approached the wick—for a moment the light of the oil lamp seemed very bright, but soon everything took on cautious, precise outlines, everything, including the naked body of the young Bride, who didn't move, remaining just as she was, and the Daughter saw it, and smiled.

It's my way of entering the night, she said. If I don't do it I can't fall asleep—it's my way.

Is it really so difficult? asked the young Bride.

What?

Entering the night, for all of you.

Yes. You think it's funny?

No, but it's mysterious, it's not easy to understand.

Do you know the whole story?

Not all of it.

No one has ever died during the day, in this family, you know that.

Yes. I don't believe it, but I know it. Do you believe it?

I know the story that they all died at night, one by one. I've known it since I was a child.

Maybe it's only a legend.

I've seen three of them.

It's normal, many people die at night.

Yes, but not all. Here even children who are born at night are born dead.

You're frightening me.

You see, you're beginning to understand—and just then the Daughter took off her nightgown, with a precise movement of her good arm. She took off her nightgown and turned onto one side, like the young Bride—naked, they looked at each other. They were the same age, and it was the age when nothing is ugly, because everything glows in the light of a new beginning.

They were silent for a while, they had to look at each other.

Then the Daughter said that when she was fifteen or sixteen it had occurred to her to rebel against that business of dying at night—she had seriously thought they were all mad—and she had rebelled in a way that she now recalled as very violent. But no one was frightened, she said. They let time pass. Until one day Uncle told me to lie down beside him. I did and waited for him to wake up. With his eyes closed he spoke to me for a long time, maybe in his sleep, and he explained that each of us is master of his life, but one thing does not depend on us, we receive it as an inheritance in our blood and there's no sense in rebelling because it's a waste of time and energy. Then I said to him that it was idiotic to think that a fate could be handed down from father to son, I said that the very idea of fate was a fantasy, a fable to justify one's own cowardice. I added that I would die in the light of day, at the cost of killing myself between dawn and sunset. He slept for a long time, but then he opened his eyes and said to me no, of course fate doesn't exist, and it's not what we inherit—if only. It's something much more profound and animal. We inherit *fear*, he said. *A particular fear*.

The young Bride saw that the Daughter, as she spoke, had opened her legs slightly and then closed them, after hiding a hand there, which now rested between her thighs, and every so often she moved it slowly.

So she explained to me that it's a subtle contagion, and she showed me how in every gesture, in every word, fathers and mothers are merely *handing down a fear*. Even where they are apparently teaching solidity and solutions, and in the end *especially* where they're teaching solidity and solutions, they are in reality handing down a fear, because they know that everything solid and solvable is only what they've found as an antidote to fear, and often a particular, circumscribed fear. So where families seem to teach children happiness, instead they are infecting children with a fear. And that's what they're doing every hour, during an impressive series of days, not letting up for an instant, with the most complete impunity, and a frightening efficiency, so that there is no way to break the circle.

The Daughter spread her legs slightly.

So I have a fear of dying in the night, she said, and I have a single way of going to sleep, mine.

The young Bride remained silent.

She stared at the Daughter's hand, at what she was doing. The fingers.

What is it? she asked again.

Instead of answering the Daughter closed her eyes and turned on her back, seeking a familiar position. She rested one hand like a shell on her stomach, and with her fingers she searched. The young Bride wondered where she had seen that gesture and was so new to what she was discovering that finally she remembered, and it was her mother's finger searching through a box of buttons for the small mother-of-pearl one that she had set aside for the cuff of her husband's only shirt. Obviously that was another region of existence, but certainly the gesture was the same, or at least until it began to be circular, moving too fast, or too violently, to be a way of searching, when it had become, rather, a way of hunting—she thought of hunting an insect, or of killing something small. And in fact, now and then, the Daughter suddenly started to arch her back, and breathed strangely—a kind of agony. But graceful, thought the young Bride, even attractive, she thought: whatever the Daughter was killing in herself, her body seemed born for that crime, it was so perfectly arranged in the space, like a wave, even her deformities as a cripple disappeared, disappeared into nothing—which was the damaged arm you couldn't have said, which of the spread legs you couldn't remember.

She stopped the killing for a moment, but without turning, without opening her eyes, and said: You really don't know what it is?

No, answered the young Bride.

The Daughter laughed, in a nice way.

You're telling the truth?

Yes.

Then the Daughter began that sonorous song, nearly a lament, that the young Bride knew but didn't know, and returned again to that small killing, but as if in the meantime she had decided to cast aside a sort of prudence that she had been holding onto. She moved her hips now, and when she let her head fall back her mouth opened slightly, in a way that seemed to me the crossing of a border and sounded like a revelation: in a flash I thought that the Daughter's face, although it came from far away, was born to end up there, in that open wave that was now turned to the pillow. It was so true, and final, that all the Daughter's beauty—with which she charmed the world, during the day—seemed to me suddenly what it was, that is, a mask, a subterfuge—or little more than a promise. I wondered if it was that way for everyone, and for me, too, but then the question I asked aloud—in a low voice—was different and again the same.

What is it?

The Daughter, without stopping, opened her eyes and turned her gaze toward the young Bride. But she didn't really seem to be looking, her eyes were fixed elsewhere, and her mouth was softly open. She continued with that sonorous song, she didn't stop her fingers, she didn't speak.

Do you mind if I watch you? asked the young Bride.

The Daughter shook her head no. She continued to caress herself without speaking. She was somewhere, within herself. But since her eyes were on the young Bride, to the young Bride it seemed that there was no longer any distance between them, physical or immaterial, and so she asked another question.

Is that how you kill your fear? You hunt it and kill it?

The Daughter turned her head again, stared at the ceiling for a moment, and then closed her eyes.

It's like detaching yourself, she said. From everything. You mustn't be afraid, go all the way to the end, she said. Then you are detached from everything, and an immense weariness carries you into the night, giving you the gift of sleep.

Then that last expression returned to her features, the head thrown back and the mouth half open. She resumed the sonorous song, and between her legs the fingers moved rapidly, every so often disappearing inside her. Gradually she seemed to lose the capacity to breathe, and at a certain point she seemed in such a hurry that the young Bride would have taken it for desperate if she hadn't just learned that it was, rather, what she sought, every night, when the light went out, descending to a point within herself that in some way must be resisting her if now I saw her exhausted, digging up with her fingertips something that the handbook of life had evidently buried in the course of a long day. It was a descent, no doubt about that, and it appeared to become at every step steeper, or more dangerous. Then she began to tremble, and she continued to tremble until the sonorous song broke off. She closed up like a clam, turning on her side, hugging her legs and pulling her head down between her shoulders—I saw her transformed into a child, all curled up, her hands hidden between her legs, her chin resting on her chest, her breath returning.

What did I see, I thought.

What should I do now, I thought. Not move, not make noise. Sleep.

But the Daughter opened her eyes, sought mine, and, strangely firm, said something.

I didn't understand, and so the Daughter repeated what she had said, in a louder voice.

Try.

I didn't move. I said nothing.

The Daughter stared at me, with a gentleness so infinite it seemed like malice. She stretched out an arm and lowered the light of the lamp.

Try, she repeated.

And then again.

Try.

Just then the young Bride was struck by the memory of an episode from nine years earlier, which I have to recount now, just as I happened to reconstruct it recently, at night. I specify *at night*, because this thing happens, where I wake up suddenly, at a certain hour of the morning, before dawn, and with great lucidity calculate the collapse of my life, or at least its geometric rotting, like a fruit left in a corner: I fight it, in fact, by reconstructing this story, or other stories, which sometimes takes me away from my calculations—other times it takes me nowhere at all. My father does the same thing, imagining he is playing a golf course, hole after hole. He specifies that it's a nine-hole course. He's a nice guy, he's eighty-four. Although it seems incredible to me at this moment, no one can say if he'll be alive when I've written the last page of this book: in general ALL those who are alive while you're writing a book should still be alive when you finish it, and this for the elementary reason that writing a book is, for those who do it, instantaneous, even if it's very long, hence it would be unreasonable to think that someone can dwell within it alive and dead, at the same time, especially my father, a nice guy, who at night, to chase away the demons, plays golf in his mind, choosing the clubs and measuring the force of the stroke, while I, unlike him, as I said, dig up this story, or others. Which means, if nothing else, that I can say with assurance what the young Bride remembered, suddenly, while the Daughter stared at her, saying a single word, *Try*. I know that what struck her was a memory she had never set aside, that in fact she had jealously guarded for nine years, specifically the memory of when, one winter morning, her grandmother had summoned her to her room, where, not yet old, she was trying to die in an orderly way, in a sumptuous bed, stalked by an illness that no one had been able to explain. Although it seems ridiculous, I know precisely what the first words she said to her were—the words of a dying woman to a child.

How small you are.

Just those words.

But I can't wait for you to grow up, I'm dying, and this is the last time I'll be able to speak to you. If you don't understand, listen, and impress it in your mind: sooner or later you'll understand. Clear?

Yes.

It was only the two of them in the room. The grandmother

was speaking in a low voice. The young Bride feared her and adored her. She was the woman who had given birth to her father, so she was unassailable, and solemnly remote. When she ordered her to sit down and push the chair next to the bed, she thought she had never been so close to her, and with curiosity she noticed that she could smell her odor: it was the odor not of death but of sunset.

Listen carefully, little woman. I grew up like you, I was the only girl among a lot of boys. Not counting the ones who died, they were six. Plus one: my father. Ours are a people who work with animals, challenge the earth every day, and seldom allow themselves the luxury of thinking. The mothers grow old quickly, the daughters have hard bottoms and white breasts, the winters are interminable, the summers scorching. Can you understand what the problem is?

Obscurely, but she could understand it.

The grandmother opened her eyes and stared at her.

Don't think you can make it by running away. They run faster than you. And when they don't feel like running, they wait for you to come back, and then they beat you.

The grandmother closed her eyes again and grimaced, because something inside was devouring her, bite by bite, each one unexpected and unpredictable. When it passed, she began breathing again and spit out on the floor a fetid liquid, colored with colors that only death could invent.

You know how I did it? she said.

The young Bride didn't know.

I played hard to get till I drove them crazy, then I let myself be caught, and then I held them by the balls all my life. Did you ever wonder who commands in this family?

The young bride shook her head no.

Me, stupid.

Another bite took away my breath. I spit out that stuff, I no longer even wanted to know where. I was careful only not to spit on myself. It ended up on the covers, not even the floor.

Now I'm fifty-three years old, I'm about to die, and I can tell you confidently one thing: don't do as I did. It's not advice, it's an order. Don't do as I did. Do you understand?

Why not?

She asked in an adult, even aggressive tone. All at once there was no longer anything of the child in her. She was tired of it, suddenly. I liked that. I straightened up a little on the pillow, and understood that with that child I could be hard, mean, and imaginative, as I had been, with great pleasure, in every instant of the life that was now fleeing in spasms of stabbing pain in my stomach.

Because it doesn't work, I said. Everyone goes crazy, nothing turns out right anymore, and sooner or later you find yourself with a swelling stomach.

That is?

Your brother gets on top of you, sticks his prick inside, and leaves a child in your belly. When your father doesn't. Now is it clear?

The young Bride didn't flinch. Clearer, yes.

Don't imagine it as unpleasant. Most of the time it's a thing that drives you mad.

The young Bride said nothing.

But that you can't understand now. Just be sure to impress it in your mind. Is that clear?

Yes.

So don't do as I did, it's all wrong. I know what you have to do, listen carefully, I'll tell you what you have to do. I called you here to tell you what you have to do.

She took her hands out from under the covers, she needed them to explain. They were ugly hands, but it was clear that if it had been up to them they would have waited quite a while before going underground.

What you have between your legs—forget about it. It's not enough to hide it. You have to forget about it. Not even you must know that you have it. It doesn't exist. Forget that you're a woman, don't dress like a woman, don't move like a woman, cut your hair, move like a boy, don't look at yourself in the mirror, ruin you hands, burn your skin, don't ever wish to be beautiful, don't try to please anyone, you mustn't please even yourself. You have to inspire disgust, and then they'll leave you alone, they'll forget about you. You understand?

I nodded yes.

Don't dance, don't ever sleep with them, don't wash, get used to stinking, don't look at other men, don't become a friend of any woman, choose the hardest jobs, kill yourself with weariness, don't believe in love stories, and never daydream.

I listened. My grandmother looked at me carefully, to be sure that I was listening to her. Then she lowered her voice, and you could see that she was about to come to the most difficult part.

But pay close attention to one thing: preserve the woman you are in your eyes and your mouth, throw away everything but keep your eyes and your mouth; one day you'll need them.

She thought for a moment.

If you really have to, give up the eyes, get used to looking at the ground. But save your mouth, otherwise you won't know where to start over from, when you need to.

The young Bride looked at her with eyes that had grown very large.

When will I need to? she asked.

When you meet a man you like. Go and get him, and marry him, it's a thing you have to do. But you'll have to go and get him, and then you'll need your mouth. And hair, hands, eyes, voice, cunning, patience, and a skillful belly. You'll have to learn everything again from the beginning: do it quickly, otherwise they'll get there before him. You understand what I'm trying to say?

Yes.

You'll see that everything will come back to you in an instant. You just have to be quick. Did you listen to me carefully?

Yes.

Then repeat it.

The young Bride did, word for word, and where she didn't remember the right word she used one of her own.

You're a smart woman, said the grandmother. She actually said "woman."

She gestured in the air, maybe it was a caress not given.

Now go, she said.

She felt one of those bites, a moan escaped her, like an animal. She put her hands back under the covers, to press where death was eating her, in her stomach.

The young Bride rose and for a while stood without moving, beside the bed. She had something in mind to ask, but it wasn't easy to find a way.

My father, I said. Then I stopped.

The grandmother turned to look at me, with the eyes of an animal in danger.

But I was a smart girl, so I didn't stop, and I said, Was my father born like that?

Like what?

Was my father born from someone in our family, like that?

The grandmother looked at me and today I can understand what she thought: that we never really die, because the blood continues, carrying off for eternity all the best and the worst of us.

Let me die in peace, child, she said. Now let me die in peace.

For that reason, on that hot night, when the Daughter, staring at me with a gentleness that could also be malice, repeated "try," which meant to remember what I had between my legs,

I knew right away that it wasn't an ordinary moment but the appointment my grandmother had told me about, while she was spitting out death all around herself: if to the Daughter it seemed a game, for me it was, instead, a threshold. I had systematically put it off, with fierce determination, because I, too, had inherited a fear, like everyone else, and had devoted a good part of my life to it. What they had taught me I had succeeded in doing. But since I'd met the Son, I knew that the last move was missing, maybe the most difficult. I had to learn everything from the beginning again, and now that he was coming I had to do it in a hurry. I thought that the Daughter's gentle voice—the Daughter's malicious voice—was a gift of fate. And since she told me to try, I obeyed, and I tried, knowing perfectly that I was taking a road of no return.

As happens sometimes in life, she realized that she knew very well what to do, although she didn't know what she was doing. It was a début and a dance, it seemed to her that she had been working on it secretly for years, practicing for hours of which she now had no memory. She let go of everything without haste, waiting for the right gestures to arrive, and they emerged at the pace of memory, disconnected but exact down to the details. She liked when the breath begins to sound in the voice, and the moments when you feel like stopping. In her mind she had no thoughts, until she thought that she wanted to look at herself, otherwise of all this only a shadow made of sensations would remain, and she wanted an image, a real one. So she opened her eyes and what she saw stayed in my mind for years, an image whose simplicity could explain things, or identify a beginning, or excite the imagination. Especially the first flash, when everything was unexpected. It didn't leave me. Because we are born many times, and in that flash I was born to a life that would later be my truer life, inevitable, violent. So, still today, now that everything is over, and we're in the season of forgetfulness, it would be hard to remember if in fact the

Daughter at a certain point had really knelt next to my bed and caressed my hair and kissed my temples, something that maybe I only dreamed, but still I remember with absolute precision that she pressed a hand over my mouth when, at the end, I couldn't stifle a cry, and of this I'm sure, because I can still remember the taste of that hand and the strange instinct to lick it, as an animal would have.

If you cry out they'll discover you, the Daughter said to her, taking her hand off her mouth.

Did I cry out?

Yes.

How embarrassing.

Why? It's only that then they'll discover you.

What a weariness.

Sleep.

And you?

You sleep, I'll sleep.

How embarrassing.

Sleep.

The next morning, at the breakfasts table, everything seemed simpler to her and, for incomprehensible reasons, slower. She realized that she was sliding into the conversations and slipping out with an ease she would never have thought possible. It wasn't only her impression. She sensed a veil of gallantry in a small gesture of the Mail Inspector, and she was convinced that the Mother's eyes *truly* saw her, even with a second's hesitation, when they passed over her. Her gaze sought the bowl of cream, which she had never dared to aspire to, and even before she found it Modesto was offering it with the gloss of two unmistakable coughs. She looked at him, without understanding. He, offering her the cream, made a slight bow in which he hid a barely perceptible but very clear sentence.

Shine today, signorina. Be careful.

The Son began arriving in mid-June, and it seemed clear to everyone, after a few days, that the thing would take its time. The first item to be delivered was a Danish player piano, disassembled, and up till then it was possible to think that a deranged fragment had escaped the logical thought that the Son had surely given to the transport of his possessions, and was preceding, with a certain comic effect, the bulk of the consignment. But the next day two Welsh rams of the Fordshire breed were delivered, along with a sealed trunk bearing the legend "Explosive Material." There followed, day by day, a drafting table produced in Manchester, three still lifes, a model of a Scottish stable, a worker's uniform, a pair of toothed wheels whose purpose was obscure, twelve very light wool kilts, an empty hatbox, and a panel with the train schedule for London's Waterloo Station. Since the procession had no obvious end, the Father felt bound to reassure the Family by explaining that it was all under control and that, as the Son had taken care to inform him by letter, the return from England was proceeding in the ways most suitable for avoiding useless overlaps and harmful complications. Modesto, who had had his difficulties finding a place for the two Fordshire rams, allowed himself a dry cough, and then the Father had to add that a minimum of discomfort had to be taken into account. Since Modesto seemed not to have resolved his laryngeal problems, the Father concluded by declaring that it seemed reasonable to predict that the Son would arrive in time for vacation.

Vacation, in the family, was an irksome tradition that was reduced to a couple of weeks in the French mountains: it was generally interpreted as an obligation and was endured by all with gracious resignation. In the event, it was customary to leave the house completely empty, and this owing to a peasant instinct, which had to do with the rotation of crops: it was thought that the house should be left to rest, so that the Family, upon returning, could go back to successfully sowing its effervescence, sure they could count on the usual abundant harvest. Therefore the servants, too, were sent home, and even Modesto was invited to have what others would have called a vacation and he interpreted as a pointless suspension of time. In general this happened around the middle of August: it could be deduced, therefore, that the procession of objects would stretch out for some fifty days. It was the middle of June.

I don't understand, is he coming or not? the young Bride asked the Daughter, when they were alone, after breakfast.

He's coming—every day he arrives a little bit, and he'll finish arriving in a month or so, the Daughter answered. You know what he's like, she added.

The young Bride knew what he was like, but not so well, after all, or in detail, or in a particularly clear way. In truth she had liked the son precisely because he wasn't comprehensible, unlike other boys of his age, in whom there was nothing to understand. The first time she met him she had been struck by the grace of his gestures, which were those of a sick man, and by his particular beauty, which was that of a dying man. He was perfectly healthy, as far as she knew, but someone whose days were numbered would have moved like him, dressed like him, and above all been excessively silent like him, speaking only occasionally, in a low voice and with an irrational intensity. He appeared marked by something, but that it was a tragic fate was a slightly too literary deduction that the young Bride quickly learned, instinctively, to ignore. In reality, in the network of those frail features and those convalescent's gestures, the Son concealed a frightening avidity for life and a rare facility of imagination: both virtues that in that countryside were spectacularly useless. He was considered very intelligent, which in the common mind was equivalent to being anemic, or color-blind: an inoffensive and sophisticated malady. But the

Father, from a distance, observed him and knew; the Mother, from closer up, protected him and guessed: they had a special child. With the instinct of a little animal, the young Bride also understood it, and she was only fifteen. So she began to hang around him, for no reason, whenever the occasion arose, and since over the years she had made herself into a kind of wild child, she became for the Son a faithful strange companion, younger, slightly feral, and as mysterious as he was. They were silent. The young Bride, especially, silent. They shared a taste for interrupted sentences, a preference for certain angles of light, and an indifference to malice. They were an odd couple, he in his elegance, she stubbornly unkempt, and if there was a feminine trait somewhere between them it would have been more readily distinguished in him. They began to speak, when they spoke, using *we*. They could be seen running along the embankment of the river, pursued by something of which there was no trace in the immensity of the countryside. They were seen at the top of the bell tower, back from copying the inscriptions written in the big bell. They had been seen in the factory, observing the workers' actions for hours, without saying a word, but writing down some numbers in a little notebook. In the end, people got used to them, which made them invisible. When it happened, the young Bride remembered her grand-mother's words and, without thinking too much about it, recognized what she had foretold, or maybe even promised. She didn't wash, she didn't comb her hair, she wore the same dirty clothes, there was dirt under her nails and a bitter odor between her thighs; even her eyes, which she had long since given up, she continued to move without mystery, imitating the sly obtuseness of domestic animals. But one day when the Son, at the end of a silence the young Bride found of a perfect dura-tion, turned to her and asked a simple question, she, instead of answering, used what for six years she had kept in reserve for him, and kissed him.

It wasn't the Son's first kiss, but in a certain sense it was. Earlier, and in different times, two other women had kissed him: consistent with the type of youth he was—ageless—they were adult women, friends of his mother. They had done it all, one in a corner of the garden and the other in a railway carriage. More than anything else, he remembered, in both, the obstacle of the lipstick. Not the first, out of delicacy, but the second, out of pure desire, had moved down to touch him and take him in her mouth for a long time, slowly, until he came. Nothing had followed from this; they were, after all, both cultivated women; but when he happened to meet them, the Son read in their eyes a long, secret drama, which, in the end, was the part that was most exciting to him. As for actual, so to speak complete, coupling, the Father, a good-natured and if necessary fierce man, had set a date for the right moment at the family brothel, in the city. Since the women there were quickly able to recognize each man's preferences, everything happened in a way that the Son found comfortable and appropriate. He appreciated how quickly the first woman of his life understood that he would do it dressed and with his eyes open, and that she would have to be silent and completely naked. She was tall, she spoke with a southern accent, and she opened her legs solemnly. As she said goodbye she ran a finger over his lips— which were bloodless, like a sick person's, but beautiful, like a martyr's—and told him that he would have success with women because nothing excites them like mystery.

So the Son had a past, and yet the virgin kiss of the young Bride left him stunned: because the young Bride was a boy, because it was an unthinkable thought, because it was a thought he had in fact always thought, and because now it was a secret he knew. Besides, she kissed in a way . . . So he was disturbed by it, and even months later, when the Mother, sitting next to him, asked him to explain to her, for pity's sake, why the devil he wanted to marry a girl who, as far as she could tell, had neither bosom nor rear nor ankles, he had one of his interminable silences and then said only: her mouth. The Mother had searched in the index of her memories for something that linked that girl to the term "mouth," but had found nothing. So she had heaved a long sigh, promising herself that she would be more attentive in the future, because evidently something had escaped her. Just then, perhaps, a curiosity was roused that, years later, would dictate on her part an instinctive and memorable act, as we'll see. At the moment, however, she said merely: After all, it's well known that rivers flow to the sea and not the opposite (many of her syllogisms were in fact inscrutable).

After that first kiss, things had rushed ahead with geometrical precision first secretly, then in the light of day, until they produced the sort of slow marriage that is in effect the subject of the story that I am telling here; yesterday, an old friend asked me, candidly, if it had anything to do with the troubles that have been killing me these past few months, that is, the same period during which I am telling this story that, the old friend thought, might also have to do with the story of what's killing me. The right answer—no—wasn't difficult to give, and yet I remained silent and didn't answer, because I would have had to explain how everything we write naturally has to do with what we are, or were, but as far as I'm concerned I've never thought that the job of writing could be resolved by wrapping one's own affairs up in a literary package, employing the painful stratagem of changing the names and sometimes the sequence of events, when, instead, the more proper sense of what we can do has always seemed to me to be to put between our life and what we write a magnificent distance that, produced first by the imagination, then filled in by craft and dedication, carries us to a place where worlds, nonexistent before, appear: worlds in which what is intimately ours, unmentionably ours, returns to existence, but almost unknown to us, and touched by the grace of the most delicate forms, like fossils or butterflies. Certainly my old friend would have had difficulty understanding, and that's why I remained silent and didn't answer, but now I realize that I might, more usefully, have burst out laughing, asking him, and asking myself, what the fuck the story of a family that has breakfast until three in the afternoon, the story of an uncle who sleeps all the time, could have to do with the sudden disintegration that is removing me from the face of the earth (or at least that's the feeling I have). Nothing, absolutely nothing. If I didn't do that, however, it's not only because it costs me a lot to laugh these days, but also because I know, for certain, that in a subtle manner I would have been telling a lie. Because fossils and butterflies exist, and you begin to discover them while you're writing; sometimes you don't even have to wait years, to reread in the cold light of day—every so often you sense them while the furnace is red-hot and you're bending the iron. For example, I should have reported to the old friend how, writing about the young Bride, I more or less abruptly change the narrative voice, for reasons that at the moment seem to me exquisitely technical, or at most blandly aesthetic, with the obvious result of complicating the life of the reader; that in itself is negligible, yet it has an irritating effect of virtuosity that at first I even tried to fight, before surrendering to the evidence that I simply couldn't hear those sentences unless they slipped out that way, as if the solid basis of a clear and distinct narrative voice were something that I no longer believed in, or that had become impossible for me to appreciate. A fiction for which I'd lost the necessary innocence. In the end it would be up to me to admit to the old friend that, although I don't have a sense of the details, I would go so far as to believe in an assonance between the occasional slip of the narrative voice in my sentences and what I've discovered in these months, concerning myself and others, that is to say, the possible appearance in life of events that don't have a direction, hence aren't stories, hence are impossible to tell, and ultimately are enigmas without a form, intended to make us lose our minds, as my case demonstrates. It occurs to me now to say to my old friend, if belatedly, that I echo the dismaying absurdity of it almost involuntarily in the handiwork I do to earn my living, and to beg him to understand, that, yes, I'm writing a book that probably has to do with what's killing me, but I ask him to consider it a rash and very private admission, completely pointless to remember, since, finally, the solid reality of the facts—which in the end surprises even me, I swear—is that, finally, in spite of everything that is happening around, and inside, me, what now seems to me most urgent is to refine the story of when, in the logical flow of their passion, the Son and the young Bride ran into that unexpected variant, that emigration to Argentina, born in the fervid imagination of a restless—or mad—father. The Son, for his part, wasn't all that upset by it, because he had inherited from the Family a rather fleeting sense of time, in the light of which three years was not essentially distinguishable from three days: it was a matter of provisional forms of their provisional eternity. The young Bride, on the other hand, was terrified of it. From her family, she had inherited a precise fear, and at that moment understood that if her grandmother's precepts had defended and saved her so far, everything would be more difficult in that foreign land, faraway and unknown. Her condition as a fiancée apparently made her safe, but it also brought to the surface what she had for years managed to bury, that is, the obvious truth that she was a woman. She greeted with dismay her father's decision to take her there with him immediately, openly useless as she was, and went so far as to wonder if in her father's sudden decision an oblique intention was concealed. She left for Argentina with a light suitcase and a heavy heart.

As we have seen, whatever then happened there—and without doubt it had happened, as we'll see—the young Bride returned punctually, more or less cleaned up, her hair properly combed, her skin clear, and her walk graceful. She had returned from far away to take what was due her, and, as far as she knew, nothing would prevent her from appearing on time, her heart intact, to collect the joy that she had been promised.

By all accounts, it would happen before the vacation.

Modesto.

Yes?

That business of the books.

Yes?

Can we talk about it for a moment?

If you wish. But not here.

They were in the kitchen and Modesto had a slightly rigid idea of the purpose of every space in that house. In the kitchen you cooked.

If you'd like to come with me, I was just going to pick some herbs in the garden, he said.

The garden, for example, was a proper place for talking.

The day was luminous; it bore no trace of the thick haze that, in that season, generally afflicted eyes and moods. They stopped beside the row of herbs, in the limited shade of a lilac.

I wondered if there might be a dispensation, said the young Bride.

Meaning?

I'd like permission to read. To have books. Not to be forced to read them in the bathroom.

You read them in the bathroom?

Can you suggest other places?

Modesto was silent for a moment.

Is it so important to you?

It is. I grew up in a family of farmers.

A noble occupation.

Maybe, but that's not the point.

No?

I went to school for a short time at the nuns' and that was it. You know why I'm not completely ignorant?

Because you read some books.

Exactly. I discovered them in Argentina. There was nothing else to do. A doctor gave them to me. He brought them every month when he traveled to us—maybe it was his way of courting me. I didn't understand much, since they were in Spanish, but I devoured them just the same. He chose the titles—everything was fine with me. It was the best thing I did there.

I can understand.

Now I miss it.

And yet in the bathroom you manage to read something.

The only book I brought with me. Soon I'll be able to repeat it by heart.

May I take the liberty of asking what it is?

Don Quixote.

Ah, that.

You know it?

A little slow, don't you think?

Uneven, let's say.

I wouldn't want to go that far.

But the language is beautiful, believe me.

I believe you.

It sings.

I imagine.

Would it really be impossible to find something else, in this house? And to have permission to read it?

Now?

Yes, now, why not?

Soon you'll be married. When you're in your own house you can do what you want.

You must have noticed that things are taking a long time.

Yes, it's an impression I've had, too.

Modesto thought for a while. Of course, he could take care

of it personally: he knew where to find books and it wouldn't be difficult, or unpleasant, to get some to the young Bride, but clearly it would represent an infraction that he wasn't sure he was prepared for. After a long hesitation he cleared his throat. The young Bride couldn't know this, but it was the laryngeal prefix that introduced communications to which he ascribed a particular character of privacy.

Talk about it with the Mother, he said.

With the Mother?

The Father is very rigid, on this point, but the Mother secretly reads. Poetry.

The young Bride thought again about the inscrutable syllogisms and began to understand where they came from.

And when does she do it?

In the afternoon, in her room.

I thought she received visitors.

Not always.

The Mother reads. Incredible.

Naturally, signorina, I never told you and you don't know it.

Of course.

But if I were you I would go to the Mother. Venture to ask her for an interview.

Knock on her door, without too many formalities—does that seem to you impossible?

Modesto stiffened.

I beg your pardon?

I mean, I could just go and knock on her door, I imagine.

Modesto was bending over the garden. He straightened.

Signorina, you know who we're talking about, right?

Of course. The Mother.

But in the same tone she might have said "in the cellar" to someone who had asked her where the broken chairs to be taken away were, and so Modesto understood that the young Bride didn't know, or at least didn't know everything, and he deeply regretted it, for at that moment he realized that he had failed in the ambition with which he awoke every morning—to be perfect—because he had granted that girl the privilege of trust without having measured the circumference of her ignorance. He was distressed by this and, for a long instant, held hostage by a hesitation that was not intrinsic to either his duties or his habits. To the young Bride it seemed, for a moment, that Modesto was actually vacillating—a mere hovering in space—and on the other hand *vacillate* is exactly what happens when we unexpectedly perceive the profound gap that is produced, unknown to us, between our intentions and the evidence of the facts, an experience I've had repeatedly, recently, as a natural consequence of my choices and others'. As I try to explain sometimes to those who dare to listen to me, I have the not especially original sensation of being nowhere, but so intensely that not even God, if, on a whim, he decided at that instant to cast an eye on creation, would be able to detect my presence, I'm so provisionally nonexistent. There are drugs, naturally, for situations of the sort, and we all have our systems for passing the time during these intermittent deaths; I, for example, tend to put things in order: objects, sometimes thoughts, very occasionally people. Modesto confined himself to inhabiting the void for a handful of seconds—many, considering it was him—and one of the privileges of my profession is to know in detail what passed through his mind, that is to say the surprising quantity of things that the young Bride, evidently, didn't know. And what the young Bride didn't know was, evidently, the Mother. The legend of the Mother.

That she was beautiful I must already have said, but I must now specify that her beauty was, in the common view, and in that circumscribed world, something mythological. Its origins were rooted in her adolescence, which was spent in the city, hence in the countryside people were aware only of distant echoes, legendary tales, details of unfathomable origin. Yet it was known that the Mother had assumed her beauty very early and, for a time, had made spectacular use of it. She was twenty-five when she married the Father; much had already happened, and yet she regretted nothing. There's no point in hiding the fact that the marriage made no apparent sense, the Father being a physically negligible man and chained sexually to obvious precautions, but it will all become clearer in the afternoon, or more likely at night, when I'll feel in my fingers the sharpness suitable to describing exactly how things went, and so not now, on this sunny day when, rather, I feel capable of the softness needed to summarize what Modesto knew and the young Bride didn't, that is to say, for example, how the trail of madness that the Mother left behind was heterogeneous, as she simply glided through the life of the city, trying out the force of her enchantment on the weaknesses of others. Two killed themselves, as everyone knows, one swallowing an excessive dose of poison, the other vanishing into the whirlpools of the river. But also a priest, who had a certain reputation, was a very good preacher, had died behind the walls of a convent, and an esteemed cardiologist had found shelter in the wards of a mental hospital. There were innumerable marriages in which wives lived, fairly comfortably, with men who were sure they had been born to love another, that is, the Mother. Analogously, at least three women, all of excellent family, all conventionally married, were known to have been so close to her, in youth, that they developed a perpetual disgust for the male body and its sexual needs. What she had granted, to each of these victims, to lead them to extremes, is information whose outlines are vague, but there are two irrefutable facts that can be trusted. The first, and apparently more obvious: the Father married a girl who was not a virgin. The second, which should be taken literally: when the Mother was a girl, she didn't need to grant any favor to cause a person to go wild; her mere presence was generally enough. If this may not seem credible, I find that I'm compelled to give an example, choosing a detail, maybe the most significant, certainly the one that has been most widely disseminated. Everything about her was magnificent, but if we talk about the décolleté, or even about the promise hinted at by the décolleté—we're talking about the bosom—then we are compelled to rise to a level that is hard to describe without resorting to terms like *spell*. Baretti, in his *Index*, to which we must inevitably refer if we wish to offer an objective outline of the situation, even hazards the term *sorcery*, but that was always a much discussed passage of his otherwise laudable work: if for no other reason than that the term *sorcery* suggests a malign intention that in no way reflects the well-known crystalline happiness that even the most fleeting glance at the Mother's bosom produced in anyone who had had the courage to attempt it, or the privilege to be able to attempt it. In the long run, Baretti himself agreed. In later recitations of his *Index*, when he was already an old man, although very respectable, the reference to *sorcery* tended to disappear, witnesses say. I use the term *recitation* because, as is perhaps not universally known, Baretti's *Index* was not a book, or a written document, but a sort of oral liturgy, at which he officiated, and which, besides, rarely took place, and was never announced in advance. On average it was biennial, it usually happened in summer, and only one thing was fixed: it started precisely at midnight. But on what day—this no one knew. It frequently happened that, because of this unpredictability, Baretti performed in the presence of only a few witnesses, if not just a pair, and one year—which turned out to be a drought year—in front of no one. It didn't seem to matter to him, and this should allow us to understand how the discipline of the *Index* was for him a personal necessity, an urgency that concerned him intimately, and others only incidentally.

He was, after all, a man of refined modesty, as one might logically deduce from his trade: he was a tailor, in the provinces.

It all began one day when—maybe to display particular kindness, maybe compelled by a sudden need—the Mother had gone to him, to adjust an evening dress that, in the city, had evidently not received the proper attention. The neckline had, as a result turned out imperfectly.

Baretti was thirty-eight at the time. He was married. He had two children. He would have liked a third. That day, however, he became old, and at the same time a child, and conclusively an artist.

As he often had occasion to recount later, the Mother pointed out to him right at the start that if he persisted in looking in the other direction it wouldn't be easy to make him understand what she wanted from him.

Forgive me, but I don't think I have the necessary boldness to be useful to you, he had defended himself, keeping his eyes away from the neckline.

Don't talk nonsense, you're a tailor, right?

I generally devote myself to male fashion.

Badly. Your business must feel the effects.

In fact.

Devote yourself to women, it will undoubtedly bring you advantages.

You think so?

I have no doubt.

I believe you.

Then look at me, good Lord.

Baretti looked at her.

You see here?

Here was where the fabric followed the curve of her breast, conceding something to the gaze and suggesting much to the imagination. Baretti was a tailor, so nudity was not indispensable to him—he knew how to read bodies under the cloth, whether they were the bony shoulders of an old notary or the silky muscles of a young priest. So, when he turned to examine the problem, he knew instantly how the Mother's breasts curved, how the nipples turned them slightly outward while drawing them upward, and that the skin was white, spotted with freckles that were just visible in the uncovered area but that certainly descended to where it was impossible for most men to see them. He felt in the palms of his hands what the lovers of that woman had felt, and he sensed that they had known perfection, and certainly despair. He imagined them squeezing, in the blindness of passion, and caressing, when all was lost: but he couldn't find in the entire natural kingdom a fruit that even distantly recalled the mixture of fullness and warmth that they must have found at the conclusion of those acts. So he uttered a sentence that he would never have believed himself capable saying.

Why so high-necked?

I beg your pardon?

Why do you wear a dress with such a high neck—it's a sin. An unforgivable sin.

You really want to know?

Yes, said Baretti, against every conviction he had.

I'm tired of incidents.

Incidents of what sort?

Incidents. If you want I'll give you some examples.

I would like that. If it won't bother you, in the meantime I'll try to operate on these darts, which seem to me completely out of place.

Thus Baretti's *Index* had its origin, first composed of the examples that the Mother generously provided, and later supplemented by extremely copious testimonies, gathered over the years and arranged in a single liturgical narrative that some called a *Saga*, others a *Catalogue*, and Baretti, with a pinch of megalomania, an *Epic Poem*. The subject consisted of the curious effects produced over the years by having touched, glimpsed, grazed, intuited, or kissed the Mother's bosom, in those who had embarked, incautiously, on one of the aforementioned five operations: what the Mother called, in a rare display of synthesis, "incidents." Baretti's skill lay in memorizing everything, without hesitations; his genius in reducing the multifaceted and infinite case histories in question to a formulaic scheme of undoubted effectiveness and a certain poetic value.

The first section was fixed:

It should not be forgotten that

Between "should not" and "be" there often appeared, for musical reasons, an adverb.

It should not, however, be forgotten that
It should not, moreover, be forgotten that
It should not, of course, be forgotten that

There followed a brief situating in time or space

the eve of Easter
at the entrance to the Officers' Club

which introduced the mention of the protagonist, most of the time shielded by a minimally generic expression

a noncommissioned officer in the engineer corps
a foreigner who arrived on the 6:42

but sometimes cited by name

the notary Gaslini

Following this came the statement of the facts, which Baretti insisted be rigorously checked

He danced the fourth waltz of the evening with the Mother, twice squeezing her hard enough to feel her breast press against the blue tailcoat.

He had a relationship with the Mother that lasted three days and three nights, apparently without interruption.

At this point Baretti paused, sometimes just perceptibly, employing a theatrical technique of which, over time, he had become a master. Anyone who has been present at one of the recitations of the *Index* knows that, during that pause, a very particular silence formed among the listeners, in which it's doubtful that anyone thought of breathing. It was like an animal rhythm, and Baretti managed it splendidly. During the universal suspension of breath, he rolled out the second part of the narrative, the critical part, the one that gave an account of the peculiar consequences of the event cited—what the Mother called "incidents." This section was less rigid: the meter had different stresses each time and the report unfolded with a certain freedom, leaving space for invention, imagination, and, often, improvisation. There was always something true, according to Baretti, but all agree with the statement that the contours of the circumstances suffered from a certain tendency toward the marvelous. It was, however, what everyone expected—a sort of final and liberating reward.

In summary, the formulaic scheme perfected by Baretti provided for two sections, of which the first (inhale) was made up of four subsections, and the second flowed with greater freedom but nevertheless respected a certain overall harmony (exhale). It should be noted that this scheme was repeated dozens of times and—as the years passed and further examples accumulated—even as many as a hundred. One can easily deduce the hypnotic or at least lulling effect of this singular recitation. I myself can state that witnessing it was a remarkable experience—rarely boring, always delightful. I mean, I've seen much more pointless things in the theater. And there I'd even paid for the ticket. It should not, moreover, be forgotten that, in April of 1907, the brother of a well-known exporter of wine, in a sudden downpour, found that, crossing the square, he was sheltering the Mother under his umbrella, who with the most natural gesture took his arm, pressing her left breast against him, apparently intentionally. (Pause.) Everyone knows that the brother

of the well-known exporter of wines deduced from it promises that later, not kept, led him to move to the South, where
at present he lives with a dialect actor. It should not be forgotten that, during the 1898 ball for eighteen-year-olds, the
Mother took off her shawl and danced alone, in the middle
of the ballroom, as if in a sudden fit of girlishness, careless of
the fact that one strap of her dress had slipped off. (Pause.)
It must also have been his age, but certainly it was there that
Deputy Astengo was abruptly stricken by a heart attack, and
died while formulating in his mind doubts about having mistaken some priorities in life. It should not, moreover, be forgotten that the esteemed painter Matteo Pani got permission
from the Mother to paint a nude of her, which, because of a
belated form of modesty, she insisted be half-length. (Pause.)
The portrait was later acquired by a Swiss banker who spent
the last eleven years of his life writing to the Mother every
day, with no response, asking to sleep with her for just one
night. Nor should it, of course, be forgotten that on the
beach at Marina di Massa, where the Mother by mistake
spent the vacation of 1904 as a guest at the Albergo
Hermitage, a young waiter who happened to come to her
assistance during a fainting spell undoubtedly caused by the
heat clasped her tight in his arms, at a moment when the
Mother was wearing a simple bathrobe over her bare skin.
(Pause.) The waiter on that occasion discovered the existence of further horizons, left his family, and opened a dance
hall where even today the entrance displays, without apparent logic, a hotel bathrobe. Similarly we cannot forget that
the third son of the Aliberti family, who suffered from a nervous condition, during a private party asked the Mother, who
was very young at the time, to strip for him, in exchange for
his entire inheritance. (Pause.) The Mother, as we know, took
off her blouse, undid her corset, and let him touch her, refusing the inheritance; the satisfaction of leaving the third son of

the Aliberti family lying senseless on the floor while she dressed was enough.

Do you make repetitive gestures? the Doctor asked me (I ended up going to a doctor, my friends insisted, I did it mostly out of kindness toward them). Not in life, I answered. It happens when I write, I clarified. I like to write lists of things, indexes, catalogues, I added. He found the thing interesting. He claims that if I let him read what I'm writing it might turn out to be very useful.

Naturally it's a possibility that I rule out.

Every so often he's silent, and I, too, as we sit across from each other. For a long time. I assume he attributes to this a certain therapeutic power. He must imagine that I, in that silence, am making some pathway into myself. Actually I think about my book. I've noticed that, more than in the past, I like letting it glide off the main road, roll down unexpected slopes. Naturally I never lose sight of it, but, whereas working on other stories I prohibited any evasion of this type, because my intention was to construct perfect clocks, and the closer I could get them to an absolute purity the more satisfied I was, now I like to let what I write sag in the current, with an apparent effect of drifting that the Doctor, certainly, in his wise ignorance, wouldn't hesitate to connect to the uncontrolled collapse of my personal life, by means of a deduction whose boundless stupidity would be painful for me to listen to. I could never explain to him that it's an exquisitely technical matter, or at most aesthetic, very clear to anyone who mindfully practices my trade. It's a question of mastering a movement similar to that of the tides: if you know them well you can happily let the boat run aground and go barefoot along the beach picking up mollusks or otherwise invisible creatures. You just have to know enough not to be surprised by the return of the tide, to get back on board and simply let the sea gently raise the keel, carrying it out to sea again. With the same ease, I, having lingered to collect all those verses of Baretti's and other mollusks of that type, feel the return, for example, of an old man and a girl, and I see them become an old man standing stiffly in front of a row of herbs, with a young Bride facing him, while she tries to understand what is so grave about simply knocking on the Mother's door. I distinctly feel the water raising the keel of my book and I see everything setting sail again in the voice of the old man, who says

I don't think, signorina, that you have available all the information necessary to be able to judge the most suitable way of approaching the Mother.

You don't?

I don't.

Then I'll follow your advice. I'll ask for a meeting, and I'll ask during breakfast. Would that be right?

Better, said Modesto. And if you trust me, he added, don't stint on prudence, since you are to deal with her.

I'll be absolutely respectful, I promise you.

Respect I would take for granted, if you will allow me: what I suggest is a certain prudence.

In what sense?

She is a remarkable woman in every aspect.

I know.

Modesto lowered his gaze and what he said he said under his breath, with a suddenly melancholy intonation.

No, you don't know.

Then he bent over the row of herbs again.

Don't you find that the mint grows very gracefully? he asked with sudden cheer, and that meant that the conversation was over.

So, the next day, the young Bride approached the Mother during breakfast and asked her discreetly if she would not mind receiving her in her salon that afternoon, to exchange a few words, in private.

But of course, sweetheart, she said. Come when you like. At exactly seven, say.

Then she added something about English jams.

Then, from the Island, a walnut writing desk arrived, followed, in order, one item a day, by thirteen volumes of an encyclopedia in German, twenty-seven meters of Egyptian cotton, a recipe book with no illustrations, two typewriters (one big, one small), a volume of Japanese prints, two more toothed wheels completely identical to the ones delivered days before, eight hundred kilograms of fodder, the heraldic coat of arms of a Slav family, three cases of Scotch whiskey, a rather mysterious piece of equipment later revealed to be a golf club, letters of credence from a London bank, a hunting dog, and an Indian carpet. It was time ticking, in its way, and the Family got so used to it that if, because of abominable breakdowns in the shipping service, an entire day passed without a delivery, everyone suffered from a just perceptible disorientation, almost as if the noontime bells had failed to ring. By degrees they became accustomed to calling each day by the name of the object—usually ludicrous— that had arrived on that day. The first to understand the usefulness of such a method was, it goes without saying, the Uncle, when, during a particularly jolly breakfast, someone wondered how long it had been since a drop of rain had fallen in that cursed countryside, and he, observing in his sleep that no one was able to articulate a plausible response, turned on his sofa and, with his customary authority, said that the last rain, which, moreover, had been disappointing, had taken place on the day of the Two Rams. Then he fell asleep again.

So now we can say it was the day of the Indian Carpet when, not preceded by the usual telegram, and hence causing some bewilderment in the happy community gathered around the breakfasts table, Comandini appeared, out of nowhere, with the air of having something urgent to communicate.

What happened, did you win at poker, Comandini? the Father asked good-humoredly.

If only.

And they closed themselves in the study.

Where, during those nights I've already alluded to, I saw them countless times, and arranged them like pieces on a chessboard, playing with them all the possible games, just to divert my sleepless thoughts, which otherwise would lead me to arrange on a similar chessboard the pieces of my present life, something I would rather avoid. In the end I knew every detail about them, as they sat there, each in his own chair, the Father's red, Comandini's black, because of those sleepless nights—I should say, rather, sleepless *mornings*, although that doesn't accurately define the fatal hesitation that dawn, too, inflicts on the sleepless, like a ruinous, and sadistic, delay. So I know every word spoken and every gesture made, in that encounter, though I wouldn't dream of recording it all here, since, as everyone knows, my job consists precisely in seeing all the details and choosing a few, like a mapmaker, who otherwise might as well photograph the world, something which may be useful but has nothing to do with the act of narrating. Which is, instead, choosing. So I willingly throw away every other thing I know in order to save the movement with which Comandini settled himself better on the chair and, shifting his weight from one buttock to the other and, leaning very slightly forward, said something that he was afraid to say, and that in fact he said not in his usual way, that is, with torrential and brilliant eloquence, but in the short space of a very few words.

He said that the Son had disappeared.

In what sense? asked the Father. He had not yet dismantled the smile left on his face by the trivial small talk with which they had started off.

We aren't able to find out where he is, Comandini clarified.

It's impossible, the Father decided, as the smile vanished. Comandini didn't move.

That wasn't what I asked you, the Father said then, and Comandini knew the exact meaning of the words, because he remembered very well when, three years earlier, sitting in that same chair, like a pawn in F2, he had heard the Father give some polite orders whose essence was: let's be sure to keep on eye on the Son, with some discretion, during this English sojourn, and possibly offer him, invisibly, appropriate occasions for deducing by himself the pointlessness of a marriage so without prospects, or sound motives, or, ultimately, good sense. He had added that a bond with an English family, especially one in the textile sector, was to be hoped for. Comandini had not discussed it then, but had tried to understand how far he could go in diverting the Son's destiny. He had in mind different degrees of violence, in the act that was to change a life, in fact two. The Father had then shaken his head, as if to get rid of a temptation. Oh, no more than a steady escort, he had explained. I would find it gracious enough to preserve a minimal *chance* for the young Bride, he had explained. And those were the last words he had uttered on the subject. In which, for three years, he had almost lost interest.

But the things keep arriving here, he objected, thinking of the rams and all the rest.

He has a series of agents, Comandini explained, scattered around England. I tried to investigate, but they don't know much about it, either. They have the orders for shipping, that's all. They've never seen the Son, they don't know who he is. He paid in advance and gave very precise, almost maniacal orders.

Yes, it's like him.

But it's not like him to disappear in this way.

The Father remained silent. He was a man who, if only for medical reasons, couldn't allow himself to indulge in anxiety: moreover, he believed firmly in an objective tendency of things to settle themselves. Yet at that moment he felt a slippage of the soul that he had seldom known, something like the opening of a clearing somewhere in the thick forest of his tranquility. He got up from the chair, and for a moment stood waiting for things to resettle themselves inside him by mechanical means, as usually happened in the case of certain discomforts he felt, especially after lunch. All he got from it was an urge to fart, which he controlled. Whereas he did not lose the sensation that he could now focus better, and review the absurd idea that the Son was disappearing not in England but somewhere inside of him, that where there had been the solid mass of a sojourn there was now the void of a silence. It didn't seem illogical, because, even though the style of the times provided for a vague, distant, and restrained role for fathers, it hadn't been that way for him, with that Son, whom he had wanted, against all logic, and who, for reasons whose every nuance he knew, *was the origin of his sole ambition*. So it seemed to him reasonable to register that in the disappearance of that youth something of himself was also disappearing: he could perceive it like a tiny hemorrhage, and mysteriously he knew that, neglected, it would expand without respite.

When was he last seen? he asked.

Eight days ago. He was in Newport, buying a cutter.

What's that?

A small sailboat.

I imagine that we'll see it unloaded in front of the gate one of these days.

It's possible.

Modesto won't be too enthusiastic.

Yet there might be another possibility, Comandini ventured.

What?

He might have taken it out on the ocean.

Him?

Why not? If one hypothesizes a certain wish to disappear . . .

He hates the sea.

Yes, but . . .

A certain wish to disappear?

The desire to become unfindable.

But why in the world?

I have no idea.

I beg your pardon?

I have no idea.

The Father felt a crack opening up somewhere inside him—another one. The idea that Comandini *had no idea about* something struck him without warning, since to that basically modest but marvelously pragmatic man he owed the conviction that every question had an answer, maybe inexact, but real, and sufficient to scatter any possibility of dangerous bewilderment. So he looked up at Comandini, astonished. He saw in his face an unfamiliar expression, and then he heard a creaking in his delicate heart, he smelled a sweetish odor that he recognized, and knew absolutely that at that moment he had begun to die.

Find him, he said.

I'm trying, sir. Besides, it's also possible that we'll see him arrive safe and sound at the door, one of these days, maybe married to an Englishwoman with milky skin and splendid legs, you know, the creator has given them incredible legs, since he couldn't dream up for them anything decent in the way of tits.

The usual Comandini had returned. The Father was grateful.

Do me a favor, never use that word again, he said.

Tits?

No. "Disappear." I don't like it. It doesn't exist.

I happen to use it often in regard to my savings.

Yes, I understand, but applied to humans it disorients me, humans don't disappear, at worst they die.

That's not the case with your son, I'm sure.

Good.

I feel I can promise you, said Comandini, with a slight hesitation.

The Father smiled at him, with infinite gratitude. Then he was seized by an inexplicable curiosity.

Comandini, do you understand why you always lose at poker? he asked.

I have some hypotheses.

Such as?

The most heartbreaking was suggested by a Turk I saw lose an island in Marrakesh.

An island?

A Greek island, I think, it had been in his family for centuries.

You're telling me you can bet an *island* at the poker table?

It was blackjack, in that case. Anyway, yes. You can even bet an island, if you have the necessary courage and the necessary poetry. He did. We returned to the hotel together. It was almost morning, I had also lost quite a bit, but you wouldn't have said so—we were walking like princes, and without even saying it to each other we felt very handsome, and eternal. *The extraordinary elegance of a man who has lost*, said the Turk.

The Father smiled.

So you lose as a matter of elegance? he asked.

I told you, it's only one hypothesis.

There are others?

Many. You want the most reliable?

I'd like that.

I lose because I play badly.

This time the Father laughed.

Then he decided that he would die slowly, carefully, and not in vain.

At seven on the dot the Mother was waiting for her, doing what she usually did at that hour, that is to say refining her own splendor: she confronted the night only in absolute *beauté*—she would never allow death to surprise her in a state that might disappoint whoever happened to discover her ready for the worms.

So the young Bride found her sitting at the mirror, and saw her as she never had before, wearing only a light tunic, her hair loose over her shoulders, falling to her hips. A very young girl, almost a child, was brushing it: the strokes all descended at exactly the same speed, each time burnishing a gilded brown highlight.

The Mother turned slightly, just enough to bestow a look.

Ah, she said, so it's today, I had a suspicion that today was yesterday, it happens to me quite often, not to mention those times when I'm sure it's tomorrow. Sit down, sweetheart, you wanted to talk to me? Ah, her, the child, her name is Dolores, I want to underline the fact that she's been a deaf-mute since birth, the sisters of Good Counsel dug her up for me, God rest their souls, now you'll understand why I have a devotion to them that at times must seem excessive.

She must have had a suspicion that her reasoning might not be completely comprehensible. She conceded a rapid explanation.

Well, never have your hair combed by someone who has the power of speech, that's obvious. Why don't you sit down?

The young Bride didn't sit down, because she hadn't imagined anything like this and for the moment she had no other ideas except to get out of the room and start again from the beginning. She held her book under her arm: it had seemed to her a way of getting straight to the problem. But the Mother didn't even seem to have seen it. It was odd, because in that house a human with a book in hand should have leaped to the eye at least as readily as an old woman who showed up at the evening rosary with a crossbow under her arm. In the young Bride's mind the plan was to enter that room with *Don Quixote* in plain sight, and, in the span of time that the Mother's presumed surprise would give her, utter the following sentence: *It can't hurt anyone, it's wonderful, and I wouldn't want to stay in this house without telling someone that I read it every day. Can I say that to you?*

It wasn't a bad plan.

But now the Mother was like an apparition, and to the young Bride it seemed that there was something much more urgent to resolve in that room.

So she sat down. She placed *Don Quixote* on the floor and sat down.

The Mother turned her chair to get a better look at her, and Dolores moved with her, finding a position in which she could continue her patient activity. Not only was she a deaf-mute; she was also nearly invisible. The Mother seemed to have with her the same relationship she might have maintained with a shawl she had thrown over her shoulders.

No, she said, you're not ugly. Something happened. Years ago you were, frankly, too ugly to look at—surely you'll explain to me what went through your head or what you expected to gain by ruining yourself like that, in what is undoubtedly a form of unjustified discourtesy toward the world, a discourtesy to avoid, believe me, so useless, the waste . . . but there is no wealth without waste, it seems, so it's not worth the trouble to . . . In any case what I mean to say is that you're not ugly, not at all, now I imagine it would be a matter of becoming beautiful, in some way, you must have thought about it, I imagine, you won't spend your life in this state, a weak broth, good heavens, you're eighteen years old . . . you're eighteen, right? yes, you're eighteen, well, frankly, at that age one can't be *truly* beautiful, but it's at least obligatory to be *outrageously desirable*, there should be no doubt about that, and now if I ask

myself if you're outrageously adorable, or maybe I said desirable, yes, probably I said *desirable*, it's more precise, if I ask
myself, then . . . get up a moment, sweetheart, do me a favor,
there, thank you, sit down again, it's clear, the answer is no,
you're not outrageously desirable, sad to say, but so many
things are sad, you certainly must have noticed how many
things are saddening if you only . . . but the earth looks different seen from the moon, don't you think? I think so, I've been
led to believe it, and so for that reason I don't think it's necessary to . . . *despair* may be a little strong . . . *become melancholy*,
there, certainly there's no reason to become melancholy, I
wouldn't want to see you melancholy, it's not important, in the
end it's just a decision, you see, you should give in to the idea,
and stop putting up resistance, I think you should *decide to be*
beautiful, that's it, maybe without expecting too much, the Son
is arriving, if I were you I'd hurry, he could arrive at any
moment, he can't continue to send rams and toothed wheels
forever . . . although now it occurs to me that perhaps you
came to ask me something, or am I mixing you up with someone else, there are so many people who want things, the number of people who want something from you is oddly . . . you
came to ask me something, sweetheart?

Yes.

What?

How to do it.

How to do what?

To be beautiful.

Ah.

She handed Dolores a comb, the way she might have read-
justed the shawl that had slid off one shoulder. The child took
it and continued her work with that. Probably it had a particular millimetric alignment of teeth that in that specific phase of
the operation had proved to be necessary. Maybe even the
material it was made of had its importance. Bone.

In general it's a business that takes years, said the Mother.

It seems that I am in some hurry, said the young Bride.

Indisputably.

I can learn quickly.

I don't know. Maybe. Do you not like to put up your hair? said the Mother. Gathered in a bun, at the nape.

The young Bride did it.

What's that? asked the Mother.

I put up my hair.

Exactly.

That's what I was supposed to do.

You don't gather your hair at the nape to gather stupid hair at a stupid nape.

No?

Try again.

The young Bride tried again.

Sweetheart, will you look at me? Look at me. So, the sole purpose of putting up your hair, gathering it at the nape, is to take men's breath away, to remind whoever is around at that moment, with the simple force of that gesture, that whatever they are doing at that moment is tremendously inadequate because, as they remembered the exact instant they saw you twist your hair at the nape of your neck, there is only one thing they truly desire in life: to fuck.

Really?

Of course, they want nothing else.

No, I mean, you really put your hair up to . . .

Oh Lord, you can also do it as if you were tying your shoes, many women do, but we're talking about something else, I think, no? About being beautiful.

Yes.

There.

So the young Bride loosened her hair, was silent for a moment, then gathered it in her hand again and slowly lifted it, twisting it at her nape and pinning it in a soft knot, ending the action by arranging behind her ears the two locks that, on either side of her face, had escaped the operation. Then she rested her hands in her lap.

Well . . .

Did I forget something?

You have a back. Use it.

When?

Always. Start again from the beginning.

The young Bride bent her head forward slightly and brought her hands to her neck to undo the hair that she had just arranged.

Stop. Does your neck itch, by chance?

No.

Strange, one lowers the head to scratch.

And so?

Head tilted back slightly, thank you. Like that, very good. Now toss your head gently two or three times while your hands undo the knot, and that will inevitably lead you to arch your back in what for any male present will signify a kind of announcement, or promise. Stop there. You feel your back?

Yes.

Now bring your hands to your forehead and gather up all the hair, carefully, more carefully than necessary, then throw your head straight back and, running your hands over your head, clasp the hair tight at the nape so that it falls gracefully. The lower down you hold on to it the more your back will arch, and you'll assume the correct position.

Like that?

More.

It hurts.

Nonsense. The farther back the arms go, the farther forward the bosom is thrust and the more the back arches. There, like that, eyes up, stop. Can you see yourself?

With my eyes up . . .

Feel, I mean, can you feel what position you're in?

Yes. I think so.

It's not an ordinary position.

It's uncomfortable.

It's a position in which a woman takes pleasure, according to the rather limited imagination of men.

Ah.

From here on, it's all simpler. Don't be stingy with the rotation of the neck, and draw this hair up, knotting it as you like. It's as if you had opened your robe and now you're closing it, simple. A robe with nothing under it, I mean.

The young Bride closed her robe with a certain elegance.

Don't forget to always let some hair escape: adjusting it at the last minute with some vaguely imprecise gesture gives a childish touch that's reassuring. To men, not to hair. There, like that, you're coming along well, I have to admit.

Thank you.

Now from the beginning.

From the beginning?

The idea is to do it not as if you had to lift up a kneading trough in the kitchen, but as if it were the thing you wanted to do most in the world. It can't really function if you're not the first to get excited.

Me?

You know what we're talking about, right?

I think so.

Get excited. It will happen to you, I hope.

Not while I'm fixing my hair.

That's exactly the mistake we're trying to correct.

Right.

Ready?

I'm not sure.

Maybe a little review will help you.

In what sense?

The Mother gestured imperceptibly, and Dolores stopped combing and took two steps back. If before she had been close to invisible, in that second she seemed to disappear. Then the Mother drew a brief sigh and, simply, pulled up her hair and slowly arranged it at the nape of her neck, in what to the young Bride seemed an implausibly expanded moment. She had the irrational impression that the Mother had undressed for her, and had done so for a mysterious length of time, sufficient to arouse desire but so limited as to prevent any memory of it. It was like having seen her naked forever and having never seen her at all.

Naturally, the Mother added, the effect is more devastating if after performing the act you are skillful enough to speak on trivial subjects, like the seasoning of cured meats, the death of some relative, or the state of the roads in the countryside. We needn't give the impression that we're really trying, you understand?

Yes.

Good, your turn.

I don't think . . .

Nonsense, just do it.

In a second . . .

Do it. Think that you are eighteen years old. You've won before you started. They've wanted you for at least three years. It's just a matter of reminding them.

All right.

The young Bride thought that she was eighteen, that she had won before she started, that they had wanted her for at least three years, and that she no longer remembered even the plot of *Don Quixote*. An incomprehensibly expanded moment passed, and at the end she was there, her hair gathered at the nape of her neck, her chin slightly raised and in her eyes a gaze that she didn't remember ever having had before.

The Mother was silent for a while, looking at her.

She was thinking of the Son, of that long silence, and his words: *her mouth*.

She tilted her head slightly, to observe better.

The young Bride remained motionless.

Her mouth was half-closed.

Did you like it? the Mother asked.

Yes.

It's a matter of *how much* you liked it.

Is there a way to know?

Yes. If you *truly* liked it, you'll now have a great desire to make love.

The young Bride tried to find an answer somewhere, in herself.

Well? the Mother asked.

I think so.

You think?

I have a great desire to make love, yes.

The Mother smiled. Then she shrugged her shoulders imperceptibly, lifting them an infinitesimal amount.

She must have made an invisible gesture, in an invisible moment, because there was no trace of Dolores in the room; some equally invisible door had swallowed her up.

Then come here, said the Mother.

The young Bride approached and stood in front of her.

The Mother stuck a hand under her skirt, shifted her underpants aside, and opened her sex, slowly, with one finger.

Yes, she said, you have the desire to.

Then she withdrew her hand and placed the finger on the lips of the young Bride, thinking again about what her Son had told her, so long ago. She ran her finger over the young Bride's lips and then pushed it between them until she touched her tongue.

It's your taste, learn to recognize it, she said.

The young Bride licked.

No, taste it.

The young Bride did, and the Mother began to understand what her Son had wanted to tell her, that time. She withdrew her finger, as if it had been burned.

Now you do it, she said.

The young Bride wasn't sure she understood. She stuck a hand under her skirt.

No, said the Mother.

Then the young Bride understood, and she had to bend over to put her hand under the Mother's dress, which was almost floor-length. The Mother parted her thighs slightly, and the young Bride slid her hand over the skin and found the sex without encountering anything else. She found it with her fingers. She moved them a little, then took her hand away. She looked at it. The fingers were shiny. The Mother gestured and she obeyed, sliding the fingers between her lips, sucking them slowly.

The Mother let her, before saying:

Let me taste, too.

She leaned forward a little, she didn't close her eyes, and she kissed that mouth, because she wanted to and because she would never miss a single chance to understand the mystery of her beloved Son. With her tongue she went to recover two things that were hers, that came from her womb.

She broke off for a moment.

Yes, she said.

Then again with my tongue I part the lips of the young Bride.

Now, so many years later, now that the Mother is no longer, I am still surprised by the lucidity with which she did everything. I mean, she was fantastic, by day, in her continuous raving, lost to herself, wandering in her words, inscrutable in her syllogisms. But I realize, in the vague clarity of the memory, how, from the moment we approached each other, just to *talk* about beauty, everything changed in her, and in the direction of absolute mastery, which began in the words and overflowed into actions. When I said that to her, at a certain point during the night, she stopped caressing me for a moment and whispered *Baudelaire's "Albatross," read it, since you read*, and only long afterward, when in fact I read it, did I understand that she was a solemn animal when she flew in her body or that of others, and an awkward bird at any other time—and this was what was marvelous about her. I recall that I blushed, when she uttered that sentence, because I felt we were discovered, I and my *Don Quixote*, and so I blushed, in the near-dark of the room, and this still today seems to me so ridiculous, to blush because of a book while a woman older than me, whom I barely knew, was licking my skin, and I was letting her, without blushing, without the least shame. She took away any shame, you see. She talked to me the entire time, while she guided my hands, and moved hers, she talked to me slowly, in the rhythm that using her mouth on me or using it to talk to me gave her, a rhythm that I later sought in all the men I had, but never found again. She explained to me that often love had nothing to do with all that, or at least she wasn't aware that it did very often. It was rather an animal thing, which had to do with the salvation of bodies. She told me that if only you avoid giving too sentimental a meaning to what you're doing, then every detail becomes a secret to extort, and every corner of the body an irresistible call. I remember that the entire time she kept telling me about men's bodies, and their primitive way of desiring, so that it was clear to me that although that mixing of our symmetrical bodies was delightful, what she wanted to give me was only a fiction that would help me at the right moment not to lose anything of what a man's body could offer. She taught me that one needn't be afraid of smells and tastes—they are the salt of the earth—and she explained to me that faces change during sex, the features change, and it would be a pity not to understand that, because with a man inside, moving on him, you can read his whole life in his face, from the child to the dying old man, and it's a book that at that moment he can't close. From her I learned to start by licking, contrary to every handbook of love, because it's a gesture that's servile and regal, of enslavement and of possession, shameful and courageous— And I don't mean you have to lick his sex right away, she pointed out, it's the skin you have to lick, hands, eyelids, throat—don't think it's a humiliation, you have to do it like a queen, an animal queen. She explained that one needn't be afraid to talk, making love, because the voice we have when we make love is what is most secret in us and the words we're capable of the only shocking, final, total nudity available to us. She said not to pretend, ever, it's only effortful—she added that you can do everything, or anyway much more than what you might believe you want to, and yet vulgarity exists, and kills pleasure, and she was insistent that I stay far away from it. Every so often, she said to me, men close their eyes and smile while they're doing it: love those men, she said. Every so often they open their arms wide and surrender: love them, too. Don't love men who cry when they make love, beware of those who take off their clothes themselves the first time—taking off their clothes is a pleasure that is yours. She talked, and didn't stop for a moment, something in her body was always looking for me, because, she explained to me, making love is an end-less attempt to find a position in which to merge with the other, a position that doesn't exist, but looking for it exists, and knowing how to look is an art. With her teeth, with her hands, she hurt me, sometimes, squeezing or biting or putting into her movements an almost cruel force, until she told me that she didn't know why but that, too, had to do with pleasure, so you needn't be afraid to bite or squeeze or use force, although the secret was to know how to do it with legible transparency, so he'll know that you know what you're doing, and that you're doing it for him. She taught me that only idiots have sex in order to come. You know what come means, right? she asked me. I told her about the Daughter, I don't know why, I told her everything. She smiled. We've moved on to secrets, she said. Then she told me that for years she had made men wild because she refused to come when she made love. At a certain point she broke off, crouched in a corner of the bed, and came alone, touching herself. They went into a rage, she said. I remember I asked some of them to do the same, too. When I felt a kind of final weariness, I pulled away and said Touch yourself. Go on. It's lovely to see them come, in front of you, without even touching them. Once, only once, she said, I was with a man I liked so much that at the end, without even saying anything to each other, we separated and, looking at each other, from a distance, not too great, we touched ourselves, each alone, but looking at the other, until we came. Then she was quiet for a long time, taking my head in her hands and pushing it gently where she wanted to feel my mouth, on her throat, then farther down, and wherever she wanted. But it's one of the few things I remember distinctly, in sequence, because the rest of the night now seems to me, as I let it return in memory, a lake without beginning or end, where every reflection still shines, but every shore is lost, and the breeze is illegible. I know, however, that I didn't have hands, before that lake, nor had I ever breathed like that, together with someone else, or lost my body in a skin that wasn't mine. I can remember when she put a hand over my eyes and asked me to open my legs, and I've often seen again, in the strangest moments, the gesture with which every so often she put her hand between her sex and my mouth, to stop something I don't know: she kept her palm on my mouth, the back of the hand on her sex. I owe to that night all the innocence that I later spent in many acts of love, to emerge from them pure, and I owe to that woman the certainty that unhappy sex is the only waste that makes us worse. She was slow in doing, childish and solemn, magnificent when she laughed with pleasure, and desirable in each of her desires. I don't have in my weary memory the last words she said, and I regret that. I remember that I fell asleep in her hair.

Many hours later the doors of the room could be heard opening and the voice of Modesto, who uttered, *Good morning, oppressive heat and irritating humidity*. He had, in such circumstances, a blind man's gaze in which was inscribed his superior capacity to see everything and remember nothing.

Well, look, said the Mother, we've got away with this night, too, I counted on it, the gift of another day, let's not let it escape—and in fact she was already out of bed and without even a glance in the mirror was heading for the breakfasts, announcing aloud, I don't know to whom, that the harvest must have begun, since for several days she had woken with an irrational and vexing thirst (many of her syllogisms were in fact inscrutable). But I stayed in bed, I who didn't fear the night, and very slowly I slipped out from under the sheets, because for the first time I seemed to be moving in a body endowed with hips, legs, fingers, smells, lips, and skin. I reviewed mentally the index that my grandmother had listed for me and I noted that, if you wanted to split hairs, I still lacked cunning and the ability of the stomach, whatever that meant. A system would be found to learn those as well. I looked at myself in the mirror. In what I saw there, I understood, for the first time with utter certainty, that the Son would return. Now I know that I wasn't wrong, but also that life can have very elaborate ways of proving you right.

Going down to the breakfasts room was strange, because on no other morning had I gone down *with a body*, and now it seemed to me so incautious, or ridiculous, to carry it to the table directly from the night, just as it was, barely kept under control by a light nightgown, and only now did I measure how it rose up on my thighs, or how it opened in front when I leaned over—things I had never had reason to note. The smell of my fingers, the taste in my mouth. But it was like that, we behaved like that, we were all mad, with a happy madness.

The Daughter arrived, she smiled, nearly ran, dragging her leg, but she didn't care, she came straight toward me, the Daughter, I had forgotten her, my empty bed, her alone in the room, I hadn't given her even a distant thought. She embraced me. I was about to say something, she shook her head, still smiling. I don't want to know anything, she said. Then she kissed me, lightly, on the mouth.

Come with me to the lake tonight, she said, I have to show you something.

We did go to the lake, in the low light of late afternoon, cutting through the orchards to arrive more quickly and at the right time, a time that the Daughter knew precisely—it was *her* lake. It was hard to understand how that dull countryside had spilled into a hollow, but certainly when it had it had done it well, and once and for all: so the water was inexplicably clear, still, cold, and magically indifferent to the seasons. It didn't freeze in winter, or dry up in summer. It was an illogical lake, and maybe for that reason no one had ever managed to give it a name. To strangers, the old people said it didn't exist.

They cut through the orchards, and so they arrived just in time. They lay down on the edge, and the Daughter said Don't move, then she said They're coming. And in fact, out of nowhere, small yellow-bellied birds, like swallows, but at an unfamiliar speed, and with other horizons reflected in their feathers, began arriving, one by one. Now be quiet and listen, said the Daughter. The birds traced the lake, flying calmly, a few feet above it. Then, suddenly, they lost altitude and descended swiftly to the surface of the water: there, in an instant, they rapidly devoured insects that had gone to seek a home, or comfort, on the wet surface of the lake. They did it with heavenly ease, and for a moment, as they did, their yellow bellies slithered over the water: in the absolute silence of the heat-dazed countryside, a silvery rustling could be heard, the feathers playing the surface of the water. It's the most beautiful sound in the world, the Daughter said. She let time pass, and one bird after another. Then she repeated: It's the most beautiful sound in the world. Once, she added, the Uncle told me that many things about men are comprehensible only if one recalls that they are incapable of a sound like that—the lightness, the speed, the grace. And so, she said to me, you shouldn't expect them to be elegant predators, but only accept what they are, imperfect predators.

The young Bride was silent for a while, listening to the most beautiful sound in the world, then she turned to the Daughter.

You're always talking about the Uncle, you know? she said.

I know.

You like him.

Of course. He's the man I'm going to marry.

The young Bride burst out laughing.

Be quiet, or they'll leave, said the Daughter, annoyed.

The young Bride tucked her head between her shoulders and lowered her voice.

You're crazy—he's your uncle, you can't marry an uncle, it's idiotic, and above all it's forbidden. They wouldn't let you.

Who else would take me, I'm a cripple.

You're kidding, you're magnificent, you . . .

And then he's not my uncle.

What?

He's not my uncle.

Of course he is.

Who told you?

Everyone knows, you call him "Uncle," he's your uncle.

He's not.

You're telling me that that man . . .

Be quiet, if you don't look at them they'll stop doing it.

So they returned to the yellow-feathered birds that came from far away to play the water. It was surprising how many details had agreed to meet in a single instant to produce the weld of that perfection: it wouldn't have been so smooth on a lake that rippled slightly, and other, more astute insects would have been able to complicate the flight of the birds, just as without the silence of the dull countryside every sound would have been lost, however glorious. Yet no detail had failed to appear, or been delayed along the way, or ceased to believe in its own minuscule necessity: so every slither of the yellow feathers over the water offered the spectacle of a successful passage of Creation. Or, if you like, the magical opposite of a Creation that hadn't happened, that is, a detail that had escaped the otherwise random genesis of things, an exception to disorder and senselessness. In any case, a miracle.

They let it go. The Daughter enchanted, the young Bride attentive, yet still lingering a bit on that business of the Uncle. The beauty of the sunset escaped them both—a rare occurrence, for, as you must have noted, there is almost nothing that can distract you from a sunset once it has caught your eye. To me it happened only once, that I can remember, owing to the presence of a certain person beside me, but it was the only time—it was in fact a unique person. Normally it doesn't happen—but it happened to the Daughter and the young Bride, who had before them a particularly elegant sunset and didn't see it, because they were listening to the most beautiful sound in the world, repeating itself over and over, the same, then a last time, not different. The yellow-feathered birds disappeared into a distance of which only they possessed the secret, the countryside returned to being obvious, as it was, and the lake mute as they had found it. Only then the Daughter, still lying down, still staring at the surface of the lake, began to speak and said that one day many years earlier she and the Son had gotten lost. He was seven, I was five, she said, we were children. We were walking through the countryside, we did it often—it was our secret world. But we went too far, or, I don't know, following something, I don't remember—maybe an illusion, or a presentiment. Darkness fell, and with the darkness the fog. We realized it too late, there was no way to recognize anything and the road back had been swallowed up by a wall we didn't know. The Son was afraid, and so was I. We walked for a long time, trying to keep going in the same direction. We were both crying, but silently. Then we seemed to hear a sound that pierced the fog; the Son stopped crying, his voice became firm again, he said, Let's go there. We couldn't even see where we put our feet, sometimes it was hard, icy earth, sometimes a ditch, or mud, but we went on, we followed the sound, we heard it getting closer. It turned out to be a mill wheel, its blades turning in a kind of canal, the mill dilapidated, the wheel straining, rattling all over the place, and that was the sound. Stopped in front of it was an automobile. We hadn't seen many in our lives, but our father had one, we knew what it was. Sitting at the wheel was a man, and he was sleeping. I said something, the Son didn't know what to do, we approached, I started to say we'd better go, and the Son said be quiet, then he said We'll never find the way home, the man was sleeping. We spoke softly, so as not to wake him, but still raising our voices a little, every so often, because we were arguing, and were afraid. The man opened his eyes, looked at us, and then said: Get in, I'll take you home.

When they opened the door at home, the Mother started shrieking something silly but very joyful. The Father approached the man and asked him to explain. At the end he shook his hand, or hugged him, I don't remember, and asked if we could do something for him. Yes, he said, I'm very tired, would you mind if I sit down here for a moment to sleep? Then

I'll go. He lay down on the sofa, without even waiting for the answer. And he fell asleep. He hasn't left since, because he's still sleeping, and because it would be tremendously sad to see him leave. It was the Son who first called him "Uncle," a few days later. He remained "Uncle," forever.

The young Bride thought for a while.

You don't even know who he is, she said.

No. But when I marry him he'll tell me everything.

Wouldn't it be right to have him tell first and then, eventually, marry him?

I tried.

And he?

He went on sleeping.

And it is what I more or less continued to do when the Doctor, in an intolerable outburst of the obvious, told me that the heart of the problem lay in my inability to understand who I am. When I remained silent, the Doctor repeated the obvious, maybe expecting that in some way I would react, for example by explaining who I was, or by admitting, instead, that I didn't have the slightest idea about it. But in reality what I did was continue to nap for a while. Then I got up and wearily headed toward the door, saying that our collaboration ended there. I recall using exactly those words, even if they now seem to me excessively formal. He burst out laughing, but it was a forced laugh, probably called for by the books, something studied, something that seemed to me so intolerable that it goaded me to an unexpected action—as much for the Doctor as for me. That is to say, I grabbed the first thing that came to hand—a table clock of moderate dimensions but with sharp edges, and solid—and hurled it at the Doctor, hitting him right in the shoulder, not in the head as the newspapers erroneously reported, with the result that he fainted, it's not clear if out of pain or out of surprise. Nor is it true that later I kicked him savagely, as one newspaper, which has hated me for years, claimed—or at least I don't remember having done that. Some extremely unpleasant days followed, in which I refused to release any statement at all, tolerating every sort of intolerable gossip, and being charged, without particular interest, with assault. Understandably, since then I've shut myself in the house, limiting my outings to the strictly necessary and sinking slowly into a solitude by which I'm frightened and, at the same time, protected.

I have to admit that, judging from the photos that came to me from my lawyer, it would seem that I really did strike the Doctor in the head. What aim.

The road was already dark when they returned, the Daughter with her Cubist gait, the young Bride with her mind on certain vague thoughts of her own.

They pretended not to notice, but the truth is that the deliveries began to become less frequent, leaving empty, nameless days, according to rhythms that seemed irrational and so somewhat inconsistent with the mind of the Son as they had known it. An Irish harp arrived, and the next day two embroidered tablecloths. But then nothing, for two days. Sacks of seeds one Wednesday, and nothing until Sunday. A yellow tent, three tennis racquets, but in between four days of nothing. When an entire week passed without a single ring from the post office by which to measure the time of the wait, Modesto decided to ask, respectfully, for a meeting with the Father. He had prepared his opening sentence with care. It was in line with the Family's deep-rooted inclinations, which were historically alien to any sort of pessimism.

You must surely have noted, sir, a certain slowing down of the deliveries recently. I wondered if it might not be the case to deduce from that the imminent arrival of the Son.

The Father looked at him silently. He was coming from distant thoughts, but he registered on some peripheral edge of his

mind the beauty of loyalty to a style, often more visible in servants than in masters. He ratified it with an imperceptible
smile. But since he remained silent, Modesto went ahead.

I happened to notice, on the other hand, that the last morning telegram is from twenty-two days ago, he said.

The Father, too, had noticed it. He wouldn't have been able
to fix an exact day, but he knew that at a certain point the Son
had stopped reassuring the Family about the outcome of his
nights.

He nodded yes, with his head. Yet he remained silent.

In the strict interpretation that he gave to his work,
Modesto considered being silent in the presence of a master to
be an excessively intimate practice, and so he avoided it systematically by resorting to a couple of elementary operations:
asking permission to leave, or continuing to speak. Usually he
preferred the first. That day he risked the second.

So, if you will allow me, I would begin to plan the prepara-
tions for his arrival, to which I would like to devote all my
attention, given the affection I have for the Son and considering the joy that seeing him again will bring to the whole household.

The Father was almost moved. He had known that man forever, so at that moment he was perfectly able to understand
what he was *really* saying, in the reverse of his words, with an
irreproachable generosity and elegance. He was saying that
something was going wrong with the Son, and he was there to
do everything necessary to see that the rule that in those rooms
did not permit anyone to give in to sorrow was not broken.
Probably he was also reminding him that his devotion to the
Son was such that no task would have seemed to him inappropriate if the purpose was that of tempering his fate.

So the Father remained silent—touched by that man's
proximity. By the intelligence, by the control. He was, just that
afternoon, measuring his own solitude and, looking at

Modesto, was aware of seeing in him the only person who in those hours inhabited with dignity the open landscape of his distress. And in fact, at moments like those, when we are called on to endure secret, or not easily expressed, sorrows, it's secondary characters, of programmatic modesty, who from time to time break the isolation we have forced ourselves into, with the result that we find ourselves, as happened to me only a few days ago, granting strangers irrational entrance to our labyrinth, in the childish illusion of being able to gain from it a suggestion, or an advantage, or even just a fleeting balm. In my case, I'm ashamed to say, it was the stock boy in a supermarket who was meticulously placing some frozen foods in the right case—but I wouldn't know exactly what to call it—his hands reddened with cold. I don't know, it seemed to me that he was doing something similar to what I ought to do, analogously, to the case of my soul—but I wouldn't know exactly what to call it. I ended up telling him. I was pleased to see that he didn't stop working while he said he wasn't sure he had understood clearly. So I explained better. My life is broken, I said, and I can't get the pieces back into place. My hands are getting colder and colder, I haven't been able to feel anything for a while, I told him. He must have thought he was dealing with a lunatic, and in fact that was the first time I thought I might go mad—an eventuality that the Doctor, foolishly, felt he could exclude, before I hit him with the clock. The secret is to do it every day, the supermarket stock boy told me. You do something every day, and so it becomes easy. I do it every day, I don't even notice anymore. Is there something you do every day? he asked me. I write, I said. How nice. What do you write? Books, I said. Books about what? Novels, I said. I don't have time to read, he said—it's what they always say. Of course, I understand, I said, it's not serious. I have three children, he said—maybe it was a justification, but I took it instead as the start of a dialogue, as an authorization to exchange something, and so I explained to him that, odd as it might seem, I could put pieces of a book one on top of the other without even looking at them, I just have to touch them with my fingertips, so to speak, while the same operation becomes impossible when I apply myself to the pieces of my life, with which I can't construct anything that has a sensible form—or even just refined, if not pleasant—and this in spite of the fact that it's an activity I devote myself to practically every day, and so many days by now that, you know, I told him, my hands are frozen, I don't feel anything anymore.

He looked at me.

Do you know where to find the paper napkins? I asked.

Of course, come with me.

He walked in front of me, in his white smock, and for a second I saw the only person who in those hours inhabited with dignity the open landscape of my distress. That's why I'm able to understand how the Father, instead of saying something about the Son, reached into a drawer and took out an envelope, which had been opened and was covered with stamps. He turned it over in his hands. Then he offered it to Modesto. He said that it came from Argentina.

Modesto did not have imagination at his disposal—a useless, if not harmful, gift in his occupation—so he didn't move: he was talking about the Son, Argentina had nothing to do with him, or, if it did, it was through connections that he couldn't chart.

But the Father was frightened by his own solitude, so he made a peremptory gesture and said:

Read it, Modesto.

He took it. Opening it, he found himself thinking that, in fifty-nine years of service, he had had access to a lot of secrets, and yet it was the first time that someone was ordering him expressly to do so. He was wondering if this would in some way change the laws of his position in that House, when the first lines carried him away from any thought. The letter was written in a somewhat labored handwriting, but with an orderliness that only toward the end yielded to weariness. It named things without seeking elegance or precision, but restoring everything to the simplicity that we imagine facts have, when we haven't had the privilege of studying them. There was no luxury, or fuss, or intelligence. Stones, if they spoke, would do so like that. It was a short letter. It was signed with a seal.

Modesto refolded the sheet of paper and, with an instinctive vocation to order, put it in the envelope. The first thing he noted, disoriented, was that there was no trace of the Son in that letter: it was something completely different. He wasn't used to confronting things in that way—he had always had the ability to arrange problems in a linear sequence, in which it was possible to consider them one at a time: setting the table constituted the most elevated example of that precept.

The second thing he noted he said aloud.

It's terrible.

Yes, said the Father.

Modesto put the letter on the table, as if it were burning hot.

When did it arrive? he asked. He didn't remember having ever in his life uttered so direct a question to the Father, or to the Father of the Father.

A few days ago, the Father answered. An informant of Comandini's wrote it—I had asked him to keep the situation vaguely under control.

Modesto nodded. He didn't love the ways of Comandini, but he had always recognized his ability.

Does the young Bride know? he asked.

No, said the Father.

She'll have to be told.

The Father got up.

Maybe, he said.

He stood for a moment, uncertain whether to go to the window, to carve out a silent pause, or to pace the room with slow steps that would enable Modesto to understand his weariness, but also his calm. He decided to walk around the table and stop, in front of the servant. He looked at him.

He told him that many years earlier he had started to do something, and that ever since he had continued to devote himself to the illusion of finishing it. He said, rather obscurely, that he had inherited from his family a tangled knot in which the thread of life and the thread of death were no longer distinguishable, and he said he had thought of untangling it, and that was his project. He could remember the precise day when it had occurred to him, and that was the day of his father's death—because of how he died, how he had wished to die. From that point he had begun to work patiently, convinced that starting would be the most difficult part: but now he understood that unexpected trials awaited him, of which he had no experience, and in the face of which his knowledge was proving insufficient. Yet he couldn't turn back, except to ask questions for which he had neither the talent nor the answers. So there was still that path to follow, and suddenly he realized that he had lost the traces because someone had moved the signs that he had prepared in advance, or confused them. And a fog or a twilight, he wasn't sure, was descending over everything. So he had never been so close to getting lost, and that was the reason that he was now, to his surprise, explaining all that to a man whom I remember, eternally, moving around my life as a child, present everywhere and always absent, so inexplicable that I was driven one day to ask my father who he was, and heard him answer, He's a servant, our best servant. Then I asked him what a servant did. He's a man who doesn't exist, my father explained.

Modesto smiled.

It's quite an exact definition, he said.

But he had moved one leg slightly toward the outside of the chair, and the Father understood that he couldn't ask that man to retrace with him the footsteps of his own disorientation. He wasn't born for that, and, if anything, his work fated him to be in the service of the exact opposite—to manage some certainties, given in life, crystallized by a family.

Then the Father recovered his usual mild firmness.

Tomorrow I'm going to the city, he said.

It's not Thursday, sir.

I know.

As you wish.

I'll take the young Bride with me. We'll go by train. I count on you to arrange for privacy, the ideal would be to travel alone.

Certainly.

Another thing, Modesto.

Yes.

The Father smiled. Because he saw the man regain color, now that he had brought him back to the surface of his tasks, after having rashly forced him into the secrets of dubious reflections. He had even put his leg back in place, lined up with the other, prepared to stay.

In twenty-two days we'll leave for vacation, he said with placid assurance. No change in the usual plans. Naturally the house will be left completely empty, to rest, as we have always done.

Then he gave a generic response to a question that Modesto wouldn't have had the courage to ask.

The Son will know how to behave, he said, however things go.

Good, said Modesto.

He waited a moment and then rose. With your permission, he said. He started on the backward steps that preceded the legendary gust of wind, when the Father, with a question, caused him to interrupt his favorite number and look up.

Modesto, I've been wanting to ask you for years: what do you do when we leave and close up the house?

I get drunk, Modesto answered, with unpredictable readiness and heedless sincerity.

For two weeks?

Yes, sir, every day for two weeks.

Where?

I have a person who takes care of me, in the city.

May I go so far as to ask what type of person it is?

If it's strictly necessary, sir.

The Father thought for a moment.

No, I don't think it's strictly necessary.

Modesto made a slight, grateful bow and had himself carried away by the usual gust of wind. The Father really seemed to feel a breeze, so great was that man's mastery. Thus he sat for a while in the brine of his own admiration, before getting up and venturing to do what, during the conversation with Modesto, it had occurred to him to do, with some urgency, amazed that he hadn't thought of it before. He left the study and combed the house to find what he was looking for, that is, the Uncle. He found him, obviously asleep, on the sofa in the hall, one of those sofas that no one reckons will be sat on—they have been added to the space to correct it, a need is feigned in order to fill a void. It's the same logic that produces lies in marriage. The Father went to get a chair and brought it next to the sofa. He sat down. The Uncle as he slept held a cigarette between his fingers, unlit. His features were free of any thought, and he breathed slowly, in the pure exercise of a necessity of life, free of hidden purposes or ulterior motives. The Father spoke in a low voice and said that the Son had disappeared, and that he could perceive him, every hour, in the irrevocable act of separating, from everyone and probably from himself. He said that he was unable to interpret it as a possibly productive variation in his fate as a man, although he admitted that it could in fact be one, because he'd never believed it would be possible to put the world in order if one allowed that some elements enjoyed the privilege of disappearing, a word he abhorred. So he was helpless, and wondered if he, the Uncle, might perhaps bring back his child, as he had known how to do so long ago, in a mysterious but punctual way, or at least help him to understand the etiquette of disappearances, since he seemed to know the details, and maybe even the ultimate reasons. He twisted his hands together as he spoke, in a nervous gesture that wasn't habitual, and that he knew came from the land toward which he was traveling, with the slow steps of his last pilgrimage.

The Uncle didn't move, but the rhythms of his presence were mysterious, and the Father waited, in no hurry. He didn't add anything to what he had said, except, as a footnote, a long patient silence. Until one of the Uncle's hands moved toward a pocket and took out some matches. He opened his eyes, apparently unaware of the Father, and lit the cigarette. Only then did he turn toward him.

All those things he sends, he said.

With a gesture he waved off the smoke, which seemed to be blowing toward the Father.

He's getting rid of them, he said.

He didn't bring the cigarette to his lips, but let it smoke on its own, as if lighting it had been a courtesy toward the thing itself.

I didn't understand it. Did someone understand it? he asked.

The Father said that it had seemed to him an odd way of returning, maybe even a good way: a little at a time. It seemed a *happy* way of returning.

Instead, he was leaving, he said.

The Uncle looked at the cigarette, gave it a few more seconds, then put it out in a vase of flowers that had long been accustomed to such usage.

Right, he said.

Then he closed his eyes. Sleeping, he added that no one disappears to die, but some do it to kill.

Of course, the Mother had opined, cheerfully, it's obvious that the girl has to see the city, otherwise how will she ever be able to understand a Gothic cathedral or the bend of a river. There were in the city neither Gothic cathedrals nor bends in a river, but it occurred to no one to point this out to her (many of her syllogisms were in fact inscrutable). It was the middle of breakfast, the toast was starting to cool, and the Father and the young Bride were in their rooms getting ready. Only I don't understand why by train, the Mother continued. When we have a car, I mean. The Pharmacist, a noted hypochondriac, and hence unusually suited to his job, started off on a reflection on the risks of travel, however one intended to do it. With a certain pride, he emphasized that he had never exceeded a distance of thirty-five kilometers from his house. It takes a certain resolve, the Mother admitted. It's one of my virtues, said the Pharmacist. And a surprising dose of stupidity, the Mother concluded. The Pharmacist made a slight bow and murmured Thank you, because he had been drinking and only later, that night, at home, reconstructed the entire sequence, grasping that something had escaped him. He hadn't slept, because of it. His wife, a harridan ten years older than he, whose breath was famous throughout the entire region, had asked if there was something bothering him. Apart from you? the Pharmacist had asked; as a youth, he had had his moments of brilliance.

So they found themselves on the train. Modesto had done his work well, and an entire car was given over to their solitude, while in the others, people were packed in amid luggage and the cries of children. It's incredible what can be obtained with a lot of money and a particular talent for courtesy.

The Father was facing backward, and this was due to the

imprecision in his heart and a scrupulous, as well as idiotic, recommendation of his cardiologist, Dr. Acerbi. The young Bride was dressed with chaste elegance, because she had decided on a fairly low profile. In fact the Mother, seeing her leave, had turned up her nose. Is she going to visit the sisters? she had asked her neighbor, without noticing that it was Monsignor Pasini. But she didn't bother choosing her interlocutor when it came to speaking. Probably she thought she was speaking to the world when she spoke. It's a common mistake. It's possible, Monsignor Pasini had answered politely. Years earlier he had fallen for a Carmelite sister, but at the moment the fact didn't occur to him.

When the train left—on the advice of the aforementioned Dr. Acerbi, they had arrived an hour early, so as to avoid any possibility of stress—the Father thought he ought to start the job that, with a certain ferocity, he had decided to tackle that day.

You must have wondered why I'm bringing you with me, he said.

No, said the young Bride.

And for a while the conversation struggled to take off.

But the Father had a mission to complete, studied down to the millimeter, so he waited for the plan to come together again clearly in his mind, opened the briefcase that he always carried with him to the city (often it contained nothing, he liked to have something not to forget on his rounds), and took out a letter. It had been opened and was covered with stamps.

I received this, a few days ago, from Argentina. I'm afraid you must read it, signorina.

The young Bride glanced at the envelope, but as she might have looked at a plate of asparagus after vomiting.

Would you prefer that I summarize it? the Father asked.

I would prefer that you put it back in the briefcase, if I really have to tell the truth.

That is impossible, said the Father. Or rather: pointless, he clarified.

Then I would prefer a summary.

All right.

The train rattled.

News has reached me from your family, he began. It's not good, he clarified.

Then, since the young Bride didn't react, he decided to push on into the heart of the matter.

You see, I am afraid I have to inform you that, the day after you left Argentina, your father was found in a ditch, drowned in a foot of mud and water.

The young Bride didn't move a muscle. The Father continued.

He was returning from an evening I don't know where, probably he was drunk, or I'd rather think that his horse shied and threw him to the ground. Probably a fatal accident, a piece of bad luck.

It's not a ditch, said the young Bride. It's a river, a wretched river, the only one in that area.

The Father had in mind a different type of reaction, and for that he had been prepared. The letter fell from his hand and he had to lean over to pick it up.

Not a piece of bad luck, continued the young Bride. He promised to do it and he did. He must have gotten drunk as a brute and then jumped.

Her voice was very hard, and calm. But the Father saw tears in her eyes.

Do you know anything else? the young Bride asked.

He left a peculiar will, written the very day of his death, the Father said cautiously.

The young Bride nodded.

The train rattled.

He left half his possessions to his wife, and the other half to his children.

All his children?

There, that's the point, if you like.

I'd like.

I have to inform you that you are not mentioned, signorina.

Thank you for your care, but I would prefer to avoid euphemisms; I know what I can expect.

Let's say that you are mentioned, but in a context that's rather . . . I would say *harsh*.

Harsh.

There's only one sentence devoted to you.

A sentence that says?

Apparently your father wished you to be cursed, for all the days that you have still to live. I quote from memory, and I apologize profoundly.

The tears began to drip down her face, but she sat with her back straight and her eyes fixed on the Father.

Is there more? she asked.

That's all, said the Father.

How do you know all these things?

I keep myself informed, any businessman does.

Business with Argentina?

It happens.

The young Bride didn't even try to hide her tears, or dry them in any way. And yet in her voice there was no hint of grief, or surprise.

Would you mind if we were silent for a while? she said.

Of course, I understand very well.

A lot of countryside went by, through the windows, unchanging, while the young Bride sat in a steely silence, and the Father stared into the emptiness, reviewing his thoughts. They passed through small stations with poignant names, fields of grain ripening in the heat, farmhouses without poetry, silent bell towers, roofs, stables, bicycles, indifferent humans, curves in the road, rows of plants, and once a circus. Only when the city was looming did the young Bride take out a handkerchief, dry her tears, and look up at the Father.

I'm a girl without a family and without a cent, she said.

Yes, the Father agreed.

Does the Son know?

It didn't seem to me of particular urgency to inform him.

But he will know.

It's inevitable, the Father lied, aware that the matter was a bit more complicated.

Where are you taking me?

I beg your pardon?

Are you taking me away?

The Father chose a firm tone; he wanted the young Bride to know that he was truly master of the situation.

Absolutely not, for now you will stay with the Family, signorina, about that there is nothing to discuss. I wanted to be alone with you in order to communicate the news that concerns you. I'm not taking you away.

Where, then?

To the city, signorina. I ask nothing other than that you follow me.

I'd like to go home. Is it possible?

Naturally. But may I ask you not to?

Why?

The Father assumed a tone that he seldom resorted to, and which he had never used with the young Bride. It implied admission to some intimacy.

You see, I was sorry to have to concern myself with things that regard you, and I wasn't happy to hear before you news that is mine only marginally. I had the vexing sensation of having robbed you of something.

He paused briefly.

So I thought I would be relieved at the idea that you, too, might learn about some circumstances that you are unaware of, and yet that have had and still have a great influence on the life of the Family, and in particular on mine.

The young Bride looked up, displaying an amazement that she had shown no hint of in hearing about her father.

Are you about to tell me a secret? she asked.

No, I wouldn't be able to. And then I tend to avoid situations that are too emotionally demanding, for reasons of medical prudence, as you can perhaps understand.

The young Bride gave a slight nod of agreement.

The Father continued.

I believe that the best system is for you to come with me where I'm taking you; it's a place where someone will be able to tell you what I feel is important for you to know.

Concentrating on a cuff link, he sought the exact words.

I must warn you that at first it will appear to you a less than appropriate place, especially after the news you've just received, but I've thought about it for a long time and I have the presumption to believe that you are a girl not much inclined to cliché, and so I'm sure that it won't disturb you, and in the end you'll see that there was no other way.

The young Bride seemed for a moment to have something to say, then she merely turned her gaze to the window. She saw that the big station was swallowing them up with its palate of iron and glass.

And what do you do in all this solitude? L. asked me, while she inspected, horrified, the maniacal orderliness of my house.

I'm writing my book, I answered.

And what did you come to do in this solitude of mine? I asked her, noting that her lips were the same as before, lips difficult to understand.

To read your book, she answered.

But with that look I know. Everyone has it, a little, everyone around you, when you've been working on a book for months, maybe years, that no one has read yet. Deep down they all think that you're not *really* writing. What they expect is to find a mountain of pages stuck in a drawer with *The morning has gold in its mouth* written on them thousands of times. You should see their surprise, when they discover that you've written the book, seriously. Assholes.

I handed her the printed pages, she stretched out on a sofa and, smoking, began to read.

I had known her, years ago. Once she had intimated that she was dying, but maybe it was only unhappiness, or incompetent doctors. Now she has two children and a husband. She said intelligent things about what I was writing, while we escaped into hotel rooms to love each other, devious but obstinate. She always said intelligent things, too, about people who live and sometimes about how we lived. Maybe I expected her to reopen the map of the Earth and show me where I was—I knew that, if she did, she would do it with a particular beauty in her gestures, because that was inevitable with her. That was why I answered her, when she wrote, re-emerging from the void into which she had disappeared. It's not something I've done, lately. I don't answer anyone. I don't ask anything of anyone. I mustn't think about it, otherwise I become unable to breathe, for the horror.

Now she was lying on the sofa reading what was printed on those pages, instead of *The morning has gold in its mouth*. It must have taken an hour—a bit more. I looked at her the whole time, searching for a name for that film that remains on women we have loved when time has passed, and we haven't ever really left each other, or hated each other, or fought—we simply separated. It shouldn't matter to me much, now that I hardly have names for anything, but the truth is that I have a score to settle with that name, it's been escaping me for years. When I'm a hairsbreadth from catching it, it enters an invisible crack in the wall. Then there's no way to make it come out.

It remains the fragrance of a nameless attraction, and what is nameless is unnerving.

Finally she stretched, placed the sheets of paper on the floor, and turned on her side to look at me carefully. She was still beautiful, about this there was no doubt.

Where the hell does he take her?

She wanted to know about the Father and the young Bride.

I told you where he took her.

To a brothel? she asked, not convinced.

Very elegant, I answered. You have to imagine a large room, lit by dim and artfully placed lamps, and a lot of people standing around or sitting on couches, waiters in the corners, trays, crystal, you might have taken it for a very respectable party, but the normality was marred by the fact that there was often so little distance between the faces—the hands initiated inappropriate gestures, like a palm sliding under the hem of a skirt, or the fingers moving to play with a curl, an earring. They were details, but they clashed with the rest, and no one seemed to realize it, or to be disturbed by it. The necklines did not conceal, the couches were tilted in precarious positions, the cigarettes traveled from mouth to mouth. One would have said that some urgency had brought back to the surface traces of a shamelessness that usually lay buried beneath conventions: just as an archeological dig might have brought to the surface patches of an obscene mosaic in the pavement of a basilica. The young Bride was dazzled by the sight. From the fact that some couples rose, and from the fact that they disappeared behind doors that opened and closed behind them, she sensed that the big room was an inclined plane and the destination of all those gestures a labyrinthine elsewhere hidden somewhere in the building.

Why did you bring me here? she asked.

It's a very particular place, the Father said.

I understand. But what is it?

A sort of club, let's say.

Are all the people real?

I'm not sure I understand the question.

Are they actors, is it a play, or what?

Oh, if that's what you meant, no, absolutely not. That's not the purpose.

So it's what I think.

Probably. But do you see that very elegant woman who is coming toward us, smiling? There, I'm sure she'll have a way of explaining everything to you and of putting you at your ease.

The elegant Woman was holding a champagne glass in her hand, and when she reached them she leaned forward to kiss the Father, murmuring something secret in his ear. Then she turned to the young Bride.

I've heard a lot about you, she said, and then she leaned forward to kiss her once, on one cheek. She had evidently been very beautiful, when she was young, and now she seemed to have no need to demonstrate anything anymore. She was wearing a gorgeous dress, but high-necked, and in her hair she wore jewels that to the young Bride seemed ancient trophies.

Because I imagined—I said to L.—this elegant Woman and the young Bride, at that big ambiguous party, sitting on a small divan, a little apart from the others, and sheltered by subdued, indirect lighting, as if enclosed in a special bubble, near the reckless joy of the others, but blown in the glass of their words. I always saw them drinking something, wine or champagne, and I know that every so often they cast a glance around, but without seeing. I know that it would not have occurred to anyone to approach them. The elegant Woman had a job to do, but she wasn't in a hurry, and a story to tell, but carefully. She spoke slowly and pronounced the names of things without embarrassment, because that was part of her profession.

What profession? L. asked me.

The elegant Woman laughed, with a lovely, crystalline

laugh. What do you mean, *what profession*, girl. The only one practiced here.

What's that?

Men pay to go to bed with me. I'm simplifying a little, obviously.

Try not to simplify.

Well, they can also pay to *not* go to bed with me, or to talk while they touch me, or to watch me fuck, or to be looked at, or . . .

I understand, that's enough.

It was you who asked me not to simplify.

Yes, of course. Incredible.

What's incredible, my dear?

That there are women who practice a profession like that.

Oh, not only women, it's something men do, too. If you observe with some attention you'll find around you women of a certain age who seem to spend their money with careless originality. Over there, for example. But also that girl, the tall one, who's laughing. The man she's laughing with, not bad, is he? I can assure you that she is paying him.

Money.

Money, yes.

How does one end up making love *for money*?

Oh, there are many ways.

Like?

Out of hunger. Out of boredom. By chance. Because you have talent. To get revenge on someone. For love of someone. You merely have to choose.

And it's not terrible?

The elegant Woman said that she didn't know anymore. Maybe, she said. But she added that it would be stupid not to understand that there was also something very intriguing about being a prostitute, and that is the reason that, sitting opposite L., who lay on her side on the sofa, looking at me, I ended up asking if it had ever occurred to her that there might be something very intriguing about being a prostitute. She answered yes, that it had occurred to her. Then we were silent for quite a while.

For example, undressing for someone you don't know, she said, must be nice. And also other things, she said.

What things?

I asked her because I remembered this lovely thing about her, that she had no shame about naming things.

She looked at me for a long time; she was searching for a limit.

The minutes before, or the hours, waiting. Knowing that you're about to do it, but without knowing with whom you'll do it.

She said it slowly.

Getting dressed without embarrassment.

Curiosity, discovering bodies that you would never have chosen, taking them in hand, touching them, being able to touch them.

She was silent for a moment.

Looking at yourself in the mirror with a man on you you've never seen before.

She looked at me.

Making them come.

Feeling that you're frighteningly beautiful, said the elegant Woman. Has that ever happened to you?

Once, one morning, said the young Bride.

Maybe even feeling despised, said L., but I don't know, maybe. Maybe I'd like to do it with someone who despises me, I don't know, it must be a very strong sensation and it's not something that happens to you in life.

And so many other things that don't happen in life, said the elegant Woman.

That's enough now, said L.

Why?

Stop it, come on.

Keep going.

No, that's enough now, said the elegant Woman.

Yes, said the young Bride.

I have a story to tell. I promised the Father.

Do you really have to do it?

Yes.

Tell me a story, instead, said L.

It was the story of the Father.

Who went to that brothel twice a month, for needs that were more than anything medical, in order to discharge his bodily fluids and assure his system a certain equilibrium. Rarely did the thing cross the emotional borders offered by a home remedy, consummated, as it was, amid the pleasure of conversation and with the purity of a tea ceremony. There were even times when it was up to the nurse on duty to reprimand the Father politely—*So, we've definitely decided to be lazy today, eh?*—while she was holding his sex in her hand, with great mastery but scant results. Then the conversation was suspended and the nurse placed one of the Father's hands between her thighs—other times she uncovered a breast and offered it to him, to his lips. This was enough to get the procedure back on track, and lead the Father to the broad delta of an orgasm compatible with the imprecision of his heart.

If all this seems irritatingly antiseptic, if not, indeed, cynical, or excessively clinical, it should be remembered that when everything started, many years ago, this story was, on the contrary, one of fierce passions—said the elegant Woman to the young Bride—and of love, death, and life. You don't know anything about the Father of the Father, she said, but at the time everyone knew about him, because he was a man who stood out as a giant in the prudent panorama of these lands. It was he who created the Family's wealth, coined its legend, and made its happiness immutable. He was the first who didn't have a name, because the entire populace referred to him as *the Father*, sensing that he was not only a man but an origin, a beginning, an ancient age, the time without precedents, and the first land. Before him there had perhaps been nothing, and so he was of everything, and for everyone, *the Father*. He was a strong, calm, wise, and enchantingly ugly man. He didn't make use of his youth because he needed to invent, to construct, to fight. When he was thirty-eight years old he looked up and saw that what he had imagined he had now accomplished. So he left for France and wasn't heard from until, some months later, he returned home, bringing with him a woman of his age who didn't speak our language. He married her, refusing to do so in church, and a year later she died, giving birth to a son who for his whole life would carry, in memory of her, an imprecision in his heart: today you call him *the Father*. The mourning lasted nine days, and so did the shock and distress, since the Father of the Father didn't believe in unhappiness, or still hadn't understood its purpose. So everything went back to the way it was before, with the nearly imperceptible addition of a child and, more conspicuously, of a promise: the Father of the Father said that he would never love, or marry, another woman in the world. He was then thirty-nine, he was at the height of his strength, his mystery, and his enchanting ugliness: everyone thought it a waste, and he was aware of the risks of a pointless renunciation of desire. So he went to the city, acquired a secluded but palatial building, and, on the top floor, had a place constructed that was absolutely identical to the one, in Paris, where he had met the French woman. Look around and you'll see. It's hardly changed at all since then. I imagine that a small part of the wealth you will come into with your marriage is from here. But it wasn't the economic side that interested the Father of the

Father. Twice a month, for twenty-two years, always on a Thursday, he came through that door, because he had resolved to carry until death a heart that would not admit love and a body that would not accept privation. Because he was *the Father*, he could imagine doing it only in a luxurious setting and an atmosphere of a communal and permanent celebration. For all that time, the richest, most ambitious, loneliest, and most beautiful women in the city tried in vain to extract him from his promise. It was a siege that flattered him, but he was unreachable behind the walls of his memories and escorted by the sparkle of his whores. Until one girl became obsessed with him. She possessed a magnificent beauty and an unpredictable intelligence, but what made her dangerous was something more impalpable and undefined: she was free, and with such unbounded naturalness that innocence and ferocity were indistinguishable in her. Probably she began to desire the Father of the Father even before she saw him: maybe the gamble attracted her, certainly she liked tackling a legend. Without hesitating, she made a surprising move, which she found simply logical: she came to work here, and waited for him. One day he chose her, and from that day on he chose only her. It lasted a long time: and for all that time they never once met outside of here. For that reason the Father of the Father must have felt that his strength was inviolate and his promise intact: too late he realized that the enemy had already entered, and that neither promise nor strength existed anymore. He was absolutely certain when the girl informed him, fearlessly, that she was expecting a child. It's hard to say if the Father of the Father contemplated the possibility of redesigning his life around that late passion and that unexpected offspring, because, if he did, he wasn't given the time to tell himself or the world: he died, one night, between the girl's legs, with a thrust of his belly, in the half-light of a room that no one has used since then. If you hear it said that it was an imprecision of the heart that betrayed him, pretend to believe it. But it was obviously the dismay, the surprise, maybe the weariness, certainly the relief at not having to invent a different end. The girl remained there holding him between her legs, stroking his hair, and speaking to him in a low voice of travels and inventors, for as long as it took to send someone into the countryside, to tell the people at home. It was all done with a discretion that had been learned by heart, because many men die in brothels, but no man dies in a brothel, as everyone knows. So everyone knew exactly what to do, and how to do it. Just before dawn, the Son arrived. Today you call him the Father, but then he was scarcely more than twenty and because of the imprecision of his heart he had a reputation as a weak, elegant, and mysterious young man. At the brothel he had been seen only a few times, and those few times he had passed almost unnoticed. He trusted just one woman, a Portuguese girl who usually worked for certain bored, very wealthy ladies: they sent their daughters to her, to learn. It was she who met him, that night. She led him to a room, lay down beside him, and told him what he was about to see, explaining everything and answering all his questions. All right, he said. He got up and went to his father. At that precise moment, the Family was little more than a hypothesis, pasted onto the unborn life of a mistake of a child and the uncertain health of a boy. But no one had understood what boy this was, and no one could know that daily intimacy with death makes one cunning and ambitious. He sat on a chair in a corner of the room, and, with his hands pressed to his heart, to protect it, he looked for a long time at his father's stony back, and the face of the girl who was talking in a low voice, her legs spread to guard a dead man. He understood that something bizarre had shifted, in the destiny of the Family, something because of which it had become difficult to separate birth from death, construction from destruction, and desire from killing. He wondered if it made sense to oppose the inertia of fate and

he realized that ten minutes would be enough to ruin everything. But he wasn't born, nor had his mother died, for that.
He got up and had them call the faithful servant who had come
with him—a man of unique dignity. He told him that the
Father had died at home, in his bed, at three-forty-two in the
morning, wearing his best pajamas and without time to ask for
help. Obviously, said the servant. Probably an imprecision of
the heart, said the Son. It's clear, said the servant, while he
approached the girl and, with an unforgettable sentence—*May
I?*—leaned over the Father's body. Displaying unsuspected
strength he picked him up in his arms. Then he made sure that
the body disappeared from the brothel invisibly, without mar-
ring the pleasure and the party that, within these walls, were
and are an inflexible obligation, always. Left alone with the
girl, the son introduced himself. He asked her if she knew
something about him. Everything, the girl answered. Good,
that will save time, the Son noted. Then he explained to her
that they would be married and that the child she was carrying
in her womb was his and would forever be their beloved son.
Why? asked the girl.

To restore order to the world, he answered.

The next day, he instructed that the mourning should last
for nine days from the day of the burial. On the tenth day he
announced his marriage to the girl, and on the first day of summer it was celebrated with unforgettable joy. Three months
later the girl gave birth, without dying, to a son, whom you will
soon marry: since then, we've all called her *the Mother*. In the
house you know, she became a woman, diligently, and she is
the light who allows that man whom we all now call the Father
to live in shadow, while he fiercely keeps the world in order.
There is something that binds them, but obviously the word
love, in this case, explains nothing. The secret they share is
stronger, and the task they have chosen. One day, when they
had been living together for a year, without ever sharing a bed,

they felt strong enough to challenge together the two fears they were accustomed to associating with sex: he of dying, she of killing. They locked themselves in a room and didn't come out before they were sure that if a spell had been cast on them, they had broken it. That's why the Daughter, who was conceived during those nights, exists: if fate wanted her crippled and very beautiful, it's no doubt in order to write a coded message that no one has yet been able to understand. But it's only a matter of time, sooner or later it will be known. When you put the world in order, the Father says, you can't decide the speed at which it will let you do so. He wanted me to tell you this story, I don't know why. I've done it. Now don't look at me like that, and finish your wine, girl.

But the young Bride sat motionless, her gaze fixed on the elegant Woman. She seemed to listen, with absorption, to words that had been delayed along the way and now were piling up, stragglers, soundless. Instinctively she greeted them with annoyance. She wondered what had happened to that day to make it so weak that it released every secret and shattered the gift of ignorance. She didn't understand what these people wanted from her, so suddenly avid and generous with truths that seemed dangerous to her. Without thinking about it, she threw out a question, biting into the words.

If the story is secret, how do you know it?

The elegant Woman didn't lose her lightness.

I was born in Portugal, I teach sex to society girls, she said.

You.

Do you need some lessons?

I don't need anything.

You don't need anything, no.

Or maybe one thing.

Tell me.

Would you mind leaving me alone for a little?

The elegant Woman didn't answer. She merely raised her

eyes toward the room, but as if she had lowered them onto a chessboard where someone had started a game whose outcome she was able to foresee, with no uncertainty. Then what she did was to take off, very slowly, the splendid red silk gloves she wore, which went up to her elbow, and place them on the young Bride's lap.

You want to be alone, she said.

Yes.

All right.

The elegant Woman rose, not disappointed, not hurried, not anything. She must have risen like that from many couches, many beds, many bedrooms, many lives.

L., too, got up, but not with the same tranquility, she wasn't familiar with tranquility, as far as I knew. She got up and looked at the time.

Fuck.

You have to leave?

I had to leave a long time ago.

You *did* leave a long time ago.

Not in that sense, idiot.

When you left you forgot a pack of cigarettes on the bed, half empty. I carried them around for months. Every so often I smoked one. Then they were gone.

Don't try anything.

I'm not trying anything.

And stop killing yourself in this shitty place that seems like a maniac's lair.

Shall I call you a taxi?

No, I have the car.

She put on her jacket, and in the reflection of a window smoothed her hair. Then she stood for a moment, looking at me, I thought she was deciding whether to leave with a kiss, but in fact she was thinking about something else.

Why all that sex?

In what sense?

In the book, all that sex.

There's almost always sex in my books.

Yes, but here it's an obsession.

You think?

You know.

Obsession seems to me a little much.

Maybe. But evidently there is something that attracts you, in writing the sex.

Yes.

What?

That it's difficult.

L. began to laugh.

You never change, eh?

It's the last thing she said. She left without even turning or saying goodbye, it was a thing she used to do then, too. I liked it.

She left beautifully, without even turning or saying goodbye, thought the young Bride as she watched the elegant Woman cross the room. I like it. Who knows how many nights it takes to become like that. And wasted days, she thought. Years. She poured herself some more wine. Might as well. The strange solitude of one who is alone in the middle of a party like that one. My solitude, she said to herself in a low voice. She straightened her spine, pulled her shoulders back. Now I'll put my thoughts in place and my fears in alphabetical order, she thought. But then her mind was immobile, incapable of setting off on the narrow pathway of thoughts: empty. She would have liked to ask what still belonged to her after that day of stories. She tried. The first thing is that I no longer have anyone. I've never had anyone, so it changes nothing. But then her mind became empty again, immobile. A lazy animal. Better for everyone to know, I can finally be myself, better also for me to know, he would have remained a father stuck in my throat all my life, better that he's dead, better now. One day I'll understand if I killed him, now I'm too young, I have to be careful not to kill myself. Farewell, father, brothers farewell. But then the emptiness again, not even painful, only uncorrectable. She looked up at the party that was crackling around her, and felt she was a shadow, in her unsuitable dress, an indecipherable move on the sidelines of the game. Nothing mattered to her. She lowered her eyes and stared at the long, red silk gloves she was holding in her lap. Hard to say if they had meaning. She took off her jacket, so she was just in her plain dress, which left her arms bare. She took the gloves and put them on, with care but without purpose, or just glimpsing consequences that were unknown to her. She liked finding a soft seat for each finger, and then pulling the red silk up over her skin, up to the elbow. It did her good to apply herself to a pointless gesture. I could learn a lot of things here, she said to herself. I'd like to return, I have to dress differently, maybe the Father will let me return. Who knows if the Daughter has ever been here. And the Mother, here, as a girl, what a sight it must have been. Glorious. She looked at her hands, they seemed like hands she had lost and that someone had now given back to her. They must be grotesque, with this dress, she thought. It didn't matter to her. She asked herself what mattered to her, at that moment. Nothing. Then she realized that a man had stopped, and was standing in front of her. She looked up: he was young, he seemed polite, and he was saying something to her, probably something brilliant—he was smiling. I'm not listening to you, thought the young Bride. But the man didn't go away. I'm not listening to you but it's true, you're young, you're not drunk, you have a nice jacket. He continued to smile at her. Then he bowed gracefully and asked, nicely, if he could sit down next to her. The young Bride looked at him for a long time, as if she had to summarize a whole story without which she would be unable to give an answer. Finally she let him sit down, without a smile. The man began to speak again, and the young Bride remained staring at him without listening to a single word: but when he offered her the glass of champagne he was holding she brought it to her lips, without hesitation. He stared at her, with the air of studying a puzzle.

You can ask, if you don't understand, the young Bride said to him.

I've never seen you here, said the man.

No, I've never seen myself here, either, she said. Nor am I seeing myself now, she thought.

The man registered the good fortune of having found an inexperienced, pure girl, a circumstance that in that sort of game was rare and presented a very special attraction. Since he knew that it was often a case of a skillful performance he leaned forward to place his lips on the young Bride's neck and when she instinctively drew back he began to think that luck was really granting him a pleasure that, provided he had some patience, would make his evening memorable.

I'm sorry, he said.

The young Bride looked at him.

No, she said, don't pay attention to me, do it again, it's that I wasn't expecting it.

The man leaned over again, and the young Bride let him kiss her neck, closing her eyes. She thought that the man knew how to kiss graciously. He raised one hand to touch her face, with a pure caress. When he pulled away, he didn't take his hand from her face and instead lingered until his fingertips touched her lips, which he didn't notice he was staring at, in surprise: then her dress stopped seeming to him so inexplicably unsuitable, and for a moment he doubted his own certainty. She knew why, and, surprising herself, took the man's fingers between her lips, held them a moment, getting hot, and

then, turning her head, pushed the man away politely and said
to him that she didn't even know who he was. Who I am? he
asked, continuing to stare at her lips.

You can make up something, said the young Bride.

Then he smiled, and stared at her for a moment in silence,
because he was no longer very sure of what was happening.

I don't live here, he said.

Where, then?

Nothing, elsewhere, he said. Then he added that he was a
scholar.

Of what?

He explained it to her, without understanding clearly why,
chose his words carefully, and with the wish that she would
really understand.

Are you making it up? she asked.

No.

Really?

I swear.

He made as if to kiss her on the mouth but she drew back
and instead of yielding to a kiss took his hand and placed it on
her knees, pushing it toward the hem of her dress, but in an
indecipherable way, which might seem insignificant, minuscule, a brief flight from a real intention. Nor did she know, at
that moment, what she was seeking. But she realized that
somewhere, in her body, was the absurd desire to be touched
by that man's hand. Not because she liked the man, he didn't
matter to her: she felt rather the urgency to throw away something of herself, and opening her legs to the man's caress
seemed to her at the moment the shortest or simplest way. She
stared at him with a look that meant nothing. The man was
silent. Then he pushed his hand under her dress, cautiously.
He asked her where she came from, and who she was. And the
young Bride answered. While she was trying to remember how
far up her stockings went and where the man's fingers would

find skin, she began to speak. Unexpectedly, she heard her own voice, calm, almost cold, uttering the truth. She said she had grown up in Argentina and, surprising herself as well, described her father's dream, the pampas, the herds of animals, the big house in the middle of nowhere. She told him about her family. It didn't make sense but I told him everything. He, slowly, with a particular gracefulness, caressed my knee, sometimes holding his palm still and moving only the fingers. I told him that what had seemed easy in Italy had turned out to be much more complicated there, and almost without realizing it I surprised myself by confiding my secret to someone else for the first time, saying that at a certain point my father had had to sell everything he had in Italy to continue with his dream. He was stubborn in his illusions, and courageous in his errors, I said. So he sold everything we had to pay his debts and start again a little farther east, where the color of the grass seemed to him right and the prophecies of a sorceress promised him unlimited and belated luck. The man listened. He looked me in the eyes, then descended to stare at my lips—I knew why. He began to move his hand up under my dress, and I let him do it, because it was, mysteriously, what I wanted. I said there were rules, there, that we didn't understand, or maybe we didn't understand the earth, the water, the wind, the animals. There were old wars that we were the last to come to, and a mysterious idea of property, and a fleeting concept of justice. Also an invisible violence, which it was easy to perceive but impossible to decipher. I don't remember exactly when, said the young Bride, but at a certain point we were all sure that everything was going to ruin and that if we remained another day there would be no turning back. The man leaned over to kiss her on the mouth, but she drew back, because she had to finish uttering the name of a particular truth, and that was the first time she had done so aloud. The men of the family looked each other in the eyes, she said, and the only one who didn't lower his gaze was my father. So I understood that we wouldn't be saved.

Continuing his caresses, the man looked at me: maybe he was trying to figure out if any of what I was saying mattered to me. I was silent, only I stared at him with a charm that hinted of challenge. I felt his hand under my dress, between my legs, and it occurred to me, suddenly, that I could do with that hand what I wanted. It's incredible how uttering a truth kept hidden for too long makes one arrogant or confident, or—I don't know—strong. I bent my head back very slightly, closed my eyes, and felt the hand go up between my legs. A small sigh was enough to push it to where the stockings ended and feel it on my skin. I wondered if I was really able to stop it. So I opened my eyes and said in a ridiculously gentle voice that my father, at night, made exactly that gesture, with his rough, woody hand—he sat beside me and while my brothers silently left the room he slid just like that under my skirt, with his hand of weary wood. The man stopped. He pulled his hand back toward the knee, but not brusquely, simply as if he had been thinking about it for a while. He was no longer the father I had known, said the young Bride, he was a broken man. We were so alone that the flight of a falcon was a presence, the arrival of a man from the crest of the hill an event. She was enchanting as she spoke, her eyes were lost in a dim distance, and her voice was firm. So the man leaned toward her, to kiss her mouth, a gesture in which not even he could have distinguished the urgency of desire from the courtesy of a protective gesture. The young Bride let him kiss her, because at that moment she was climbing back up the slope of truth, and any other gesture was indifferent to her—it was somewhere else that she was going. She barely felt the man's tongue, it didn't matter to her. She felt, but peripherally, that that hand, under her dress, was approaching her sex. She pulled away from the man's mouth and said that in the end the only solution that could be found was to come to an agreement with certain people, down there, and this meant that she would have had to marry a man she scarcely knew. He wasn't even an unpleasant man, the young Bride smiled, but I was engaged to a youth I loved, here in Italy. Whom I love, I said. I barely opened my legs and let the man's fingers find my sex. So I said to my father that I would never do it, and that I would leave, as it had long since been decided, to marry here, and nothing could keep me from going. He said that I would ruin him. He said that if I left he would kill himself the next day. The man opened my sex with his fingers. I said that I ran away at night, with the help of my brothers, and that I didn't turn around until I had crossed the ocean. And when the man put his fingers in my sex I said that my father, the day after I fled, had killed himself. The man stopped. They say he was drunk and fell into a river, I added, but I know that he shot himself in the head with his gun, because he had described to me exactly how he would do it, and had promised me that, at the last moment, he would have neither fear nor regrets. Then the man looked me in the eyes, he wanted to know what was happening. I took his hand gently and drew it out from under my dress. I brought it to my mouth and took his fingers between my lips, for a moment. Then I said that I would be infinitely grateful if he would be so kind as to leave me alone. He looked at me without understanding. I would be infinitely grateful if you would now be so kind as to leave me alone, the young Bride repeated. The man asked a question. Please, said the young Bride. Then the man rose, an instinct made reflexive by his upbringing and without understanding what had happened to him. He uttered some civility, but then he stood there, to prolong something he didn't know. Finally he said that that wasn't the most suitable way to entertain a man in that place. I can't say you're wrong and I beg you to accept my apologies, said the young Bride: but calmly, without the shadow of a regret. The man left with a bow. Many times, in his life, he would try to forget that encounter, without being able to, or to describe it to someone, without finding the right words.

They look nice, said the Father, indicating the long red gloves.

The young Bride adjusted a fold of her dress.

They're not mine, she said.

Too bad. Shall we go?

They returned on the train, again alone, sitting opposite each other, in the light of a long sunset, and, thinking back on it now, I can recall in detail, despite all the years that have passed, the purpose with which, my back straight, not even leaning against the seat, I was proud of fighting an immense weariness. It was pride, but of a type that the blood generates only in youth—coupling it, mistakenly, with weakness. The jolting of the train kept me awake, along with the suspicion that a defining infamy had, all in one day, been poured into the hollow of my life, as into a cup that now seemed impossible to empty: I managed to tip it just enough to see the opaque liquid of shame drain from the edges—I felt it running slowly, without knowing what to think. If I had been clearheaded, if I had had a thousand lives more, I would have known instead that that strange day, of confessions and bizarre events, had offered a lesson that took me years, and many mistakes, to learn. In every detail, what I had done in those hours—and heard, and said, and seen—was teaching me that it's bodies that dictate life: the rest is a result. I couldn't believe it, at that moment, because, like every young person, I expected something more complex, or sophisticated. But now I don't know any story, mine or anyone else's, that did not begin in the animal movement of a body—an inclination, a wound, an obliqueness, at times a brilliant move, often obscene instincts that came from far away. It's all written there already. The thoughts come afterward, and are always a belated map, to which, out of convention and weariness, we attribute some precision. Probably it was what the Father intended to explain to me, with the apparently absurd act of taking a girl to a brothel. At the distance of years, I have to acknowledge in him a courageous exactness. He wanted to take me to a place where it was impossible to protect oneself from the truth—and inevitable to hear it. He had to tell me that the weave of destinies that the loom of our families had worked on for years had been made with a primitive, animal thread. And that, however we might strive to seek more elegant or artificial explanations, for all of us our origin was written in our bodies, in characters engraved with fire—whether it was the imprecision of a heart, the scandal of reckless beauty, or the brutal necessity of desire. Thus we live in the illusion that we are putting back in order what the humiliating or marvelous act of a body has thrown into disarray. In a final marvelous or humiliating act of the body, we die. All the rest is a useless dance, made memorable by wonderful dancers. But I know it now, I didn't know it then—and on the train I was too tired to understand it, or proud, or frightened, I don't know. I sat with my back straight and that was everything. I looked at the Father: the features of a good-natured man, a secondary character, had returned—he sat with his hands entwined, resting in his lap, and stared at them. Every so often, he raised his eyes to the window, but briefly. Then he went back to staring at his hands. A performance. The young Bride realized that she found that man, suddenly, irresistible, putting together what she had learned about him and the unassuming figure now facing her. She noted for the first time the Father's spectacular ability to hide the strength he had available, the illusions he was capable of, and the boundless ambition to which he was devoting his life. A professional gambler, who won with invisible cards. A fantastic cardsharp. She saw in him a beauty that not for an instant had she suspected, before that day. She liked that solitude, in the moving train, and the fact of having been *the two of them*, for a day. She was eighteen: she got up, went to sit next to him, and when she realized that he wouldn't stop staring at his hands, she leaned her head on his shoulder and fell asleep.

The Father interpreted it as a gesture of summing up, the compendium of everything that the young Bride might have thought about what she had learned that day. It seemed to him even to have a particular, unexpected precision. So he let her sleep and went back to what he was doing, staring at his hands. He was considering the actions that had been accomplished that day, drawing from them the placid satisfaction of a general who, in altering the disposition of troops on the battlefield, had obtained an arrangement more suited to the terrain and less vulnerable to the inventions of the enemy. There were naturally some details to work out, first among them finding the Son who had disappeared, but the harvest of that day of grand maneuvers inclined him to optimism. Having reached these conclusions, he stopped staring at his hands and, looking out the window, allowed himself a ritual of the mind that he had been unable to perform for some time: reviewing his own certainties. He had a number, and of different types. He mixed them up with childish pleasure. He started from an idea, about which he had no doubts, that in summer it was advisable to use shaving cream perfumed with citrus. Then he continued with the conviction, developed over the years, that cashmere does not in fact exist, and continued by repeating the obvious evidence of the nonexistence of God. When he realized that it was time to get off, he jumped to the last certainty on the list, because it was the one that he cared about most, the only one that he had never confided to anyone, and for which he reserved the most heroic part of himself. He never thought it without uttering it aloud.

I won't die at night, I will die in the light of the sun.

The young Bride raised her head from his shoulder, coming from distant dreams.

Did you say something?

That we have to get off, signorina.

When they left the station the young Bride still hadn't said anything, caught in the spiderweb of a complicated awakening. Modesto had come to get them in a carriage and he drove them home, noting the little news of the day with a shade of lightness in his voice: it was standard in the Family, in fact, for any return, even the most predictable, to bring joy to manners and relief to gestures.

Only when they had got out of the carriage, and just a few steps divided them from the threshold of the house, the young Bride took the Father by the arm and stopped. Infallible, Modesto continued, without turning, and disappeared into a side door. The young Bride clutched the Father's arm but without shifting her gaze from the broad pale façade that was about to swallow them up.

And now? she asked.

The Father was unruffled.

We'll do what has to be done, he said.

Which is?

What a question. We'll go on vacation, my dear.

Not when I wrote it but days later when, lying on the sofa, I reread it, I noticed that sentence I had written, and started looking at it more closely. If you wanted, you could even try to refine it a bit. For example, *It will be day, in the light of the sun, when I die* sounded more sonorous. Also, *I wish to die in the light of the sun, and I will* might work. When it's like that I try to read the sentence out loud—after all, the Father said it out loud—and repeating it, then, I listened to it, and suddenly it was as if I hadn't written it but received it, right at that moment, as if it had drifted here from some unknown distance. It happens. The sound was clear, the posture correct. *I will not die at night, I will die in the light of the sun.* It didn't come from me, it was there, that's all: so I realized that it said something that I wouldn't have been able to formulate but that I now recognized with assurance. It had to do with me. I read it again and understood, in all simplicity, that what was left for me to desire, since my bewilderment is a given, was in fact to die in the light of the sun, although *die* was undoubtedly a rather hasty term—let's say *disappear*. But not at night, that was now clear to me. In the light of the sun. I was lying on the sofa, I repeat, and was engaged in the only activity that I've been able to do lately with confidence and with control, that is to say, write a book: but suddenly I was no longer writing, I was *living*—the very thing that I've neglected to do for some time, or at least whenever it's possible—if *living* is the name of that rapid return to oneself that I experienced, without warning, while, lying on the sofa, I was reading aloud a sentence that I had written some days earlier and that now appeared to me, as if coming from afar, in the convincing light of a voice that was no longer mine.

I looked around. The things, the orderliness, the half-light. The lair of a maniac, L. had said. A little exaggerated, as usual. And yet.

Is it possible that it has to end like this?

Occasionally—as has surely been noted—I happen to think: is it possible that it has to end like this?

For my part, it was a while since I'd thought it. I had stopped interrogating myself. We slide down, without noticing much, deafened by grief, and that's all.

But at that moment I thought—*Is it possible that it has to end like this?*—and it was clear to me that, whatever the destination of my life, the light in which I was waiting to know it was certainly inappropriate, as the landscape in which I allowed it to approach was absurd, and the rigidity that I had reserved for the wait was demented. It was all unfair.

On the turn that my affair had taken I didn't dare to pass judgment. But as for the décor, I had something to say.

I will not die at night, I will die in the light of the sun.

That was what I had to say.

Honestly, I would never have expected such a burst of determination and I'm still amazed that what generated it was a sentence read in a book (that it was a book of *mine* is undoubtedly a rather painful detail). What I can say is that I took the thing literally—I will not die at night, I will die in the light of the sun—since I had long since lost the energy, or the imagination, to elaborate the thing symbolically, as no doubt the Doctor would have demanded of me (among other things, it has been determined that I owe him twelve thousand euros), surely pushing me to translate the term "light" into a new disposition of the spirit and the term "night" into the projection of my blind fantasies: bullshit. I resolved, more simply—and not having available, as I said, the energy and imagination needed for a different solution—to go to the sea. No, not really—I'm not so lacking in energy and imagination, after all. But it's true that, instead of imagining who knows what, I was able only to go back to a morning years ago and a ferry that, in winter light, carried me to an island. It was in the south. The speed was slow, the sea calm. If you sat on the proper side of the bridge, you would travel with the sun in your eyes, but since it was a morning in February you were just bathed by the light. The muffled sound of the engines was a comfort.

It must still exist, I said to myself. I was thinking of the ferry.

It was a matter of reconstructing some details that now escaped me (what island? for example), but naturally we're speaking of negligible obstacles, and that's the reason that, with a determination that now still amazes me, I got off the couch to get on that ferry, though I was perfectly aware of the uncertain series of movements that going from one to the other would involve (it's miraculous, on the other hand, how, in the formal simplicity of the written sentence, "couch" and "ferry" are practically attached: this is the primacy of writing over living, as I will never get tired of repeating). I remember that I took leave of my apartment in twenty minutes—and more generally from a particular apparatus of partial certainties, and ultimately from the organized darkness in which I had buried myself. If one had an idea of how little is required to dismantle them, one would never waste so much time building strategic defenses against the insults of life. There was enough time to choose the few objects to take away—the number eleven occurred to me. Eleven objects, then—choosing them was a delight. I did it while, at a similar pace, the Family, in my head, sailed toward vacation, in a broad collective movement that later was a pleasure to fix in the clear lines of the writing, at a table in a tiny hotel, the first on the road south, during the first night after eternity. Having to arrange things in an orderly fashion, I began by remembering how the vacation, for all of them, represented an irritating problem that was resolved by a couple of weeks spent in the French mountains: I don't know exactly where, but I must have already said that it was generally interpreted as an obligation, and so borne by all with gracious resignation.

To reduce the annoyance to a minimum, they resorted to fragile expedients, the most curious of which was to avoid packing suitcases: they would buy everything when they got there. The only one who had trunks, and insisted on using them, was the Uncle, who liked to take with him, without pointless half measures, everything he possessed. He packed himself: given that he did it sleeping, the thing could take weeks. All the others, on the contrary, applied themselves the morning of the departure, setting aside objects of dubious usefulness in small purses that they then often forgot. There were some constants: the Mother, for example, never left without her pillow, some postcards that on earlier trips she hadn't had time to write, lavender sachets, and the score of a French song whose last page was missing. The Father was set on taking a chess handbook, the Daughter an album and oil paints (for mysterious reasons she left at home the colors from azure to blue). The Son, in the days before he disappeared, took apart the clock on the stairs and brought the pieces, promising himself to put it back together during the vacation. The final result of such a selection of objects was a moderate number of bags and a certain sum total of regrets: it was often necessary to leave at home precious fragments of the common folly.

Modesto saw to the house. There, too, faithfulness was maintained to a protocol whose rationale, if it existed, was rooted in a past that could no longer provide explanations. All the furniture was covered with linen sheets, the pantries were filled with every nonperishable food item, the shutters were half closed, except those facing south; the carpets were rolled up, the paintings were taken off the walls and placed on the floor (there was a reason but it had been lost), the clocks were allowed to wind down, yellow flowers were placed in every vase, the table was set for a breakfast for twenty-five people, the wheels were taken off everything that had wheels, and all the garments that, in the course of the past year, had not been worn at least once were thrown away. Particular care was reserved for the treasured rite of leaving half-finished acts scattered throughout the house: it seemed a sure guarantee that they would return to complete them. Thus, once the Family had left, the rooms offered to an attentive gaze a whole storm of activities abandoned midway through: a soapy shaving brush, card games left at the crucial moment, basins full of water, half-peeled fruit, a cup of tea still to be drunk. On the piano a score was usually open to the next-to-last page, and an unfinished letter always remained on the Mother's desk. Hanging on the kitchen wall was an apparently urgent shopping list, in the drawers exquisite crochet works were left uncompleted, and on the billiard table a sublime shot was inexplicably put off. In the air, if one could have seen them, hovered thoughts broken off in the middle, incomplete memories, illusions to perfect, and poems without endings: it was thought that fate could see them. The picture was completed, at the moment of departure, when a good part of the baggage was left, forgotten, in the halls—a gesture that was painful but considered crucial. In the light of such dedication, the possibility that the dangers of the journey might cause any of them not to return home was considered simply offensive.

It took a certain amount of time to carry out all these tasks. So the family began preparing for the departure well in advance, gently aligning the daily dictation of activities with the target represented by THE DAY OF DEPARTURE. In practice, it meant that each one continued to do exactly the same things, adding to gestures an extra precariousness generated by the imminence of leave-taking, and removing from thoughts any residual dramatic tone, made useless by the approaching spiritual amnesty. Only the Uncle, as noted, proceeded with large-scale works (packing the trunks). For the rest, the imminence of THE DAY OF DEPARTURE was made tangible by the feverish activity of the staff, an octopus of which Modesto represented the head and the more negligible servants the tentacles. The mandate was to do everything with great refinement but without useless hesitation. Given that, for example, owing to an inexplicable custom, all the pillows in the house were removed and assembled in a single wardrobe, the least that could happen was that the thin cushion that softened the wicker of the chairs around the table for breakfasts would be removed, with a certain style, from under your rear: in that case, you didn't even break off the conversation, you simply raised yourself slightly, as if you had an urgent need to release gas, and let the servants complete their task. In the same way they might cause a sugar bowl to vanish, or shoes, or, in especially dramatic cases, entire rooms: you suddenly discovered that the use of the stairs had been suspended. So, while its inhabitants continued to dismiss the deadline that awaited them, placing THE DAY OF DEPARTURE in a near future with uncertain borders, the house proceeded inexorably toward the goal: a sort of double velocity emerged—one of the spirit, the other of the things—that opened the tranquility of the days to the incursion of surreal dissymmetries. There were people who, without blinking an eye, sat at tables that were no longer there, guests who arrived late for events that were still to happen, mirrors that, removed from their positions, reflected events of hours earlier, and noises that, remaining in the air, orphaned of their origins, wandered through the rooms until Modesto saw to relocating them, temporarily, in drawers that were later marked with a red painted cross. (Seldom, upon returning, did anyone remember to release them. The family preferred to do it, as a game, during Carnival: then, sometimes, friends or acquaintances appeared who, belatedly, came by to retrieve a particular sentence or a bodily noise that had been lost the preceding summer. Lawyer Squinzi, to take just one example, managed to recover a burp from the previous year in a drawer where, to his surprise, he also found a hysterical laugh of his wife's and the start of a hailstorm that, at the time, had made the price of peaches take off. Don Giustelli, an excellent man of the Lord whom I had the good fortune to know and to see regularly, confessed to me once that he used to show up at the opening of the drawers to corner the market in answers. You know, there were a lot of them inside there, he told me. I became persuaded, he found a way of explaining, that in the period preceding THE DAY OF DEPARTURE, in that house, many answers were lost in conversation, because one paid less attention (at times no attention)—so they were lost. They remained in the air, that was known: and later ended up in the famous drawers. Usually, Don Giustelli added, in

February I had already used up my supply of answers, so of course it was convenient to go and retrieve some from those drawers, and without spending a cent, besides. All answers of excellent quality, he emphasized. In fact, when he wished to show me some, I had to agree that the formal quality was almost always superior to the norm. There were some that were splendidly terse—*never, forever*—and no shortage of ones endowed with a kind of elegant musicality: *not in revenge, if anything out of astonishment, at most by chance.* (I, personally, however, found those answers *agonizing*. The fact that you could no longer link them to any question was obviously intolerable. It wasn't only my problem. Some years ago, the youngest daughter of the Ballards, then twenty, appeared at the opening of the drawers to retrieve a guitar chord that had made her dream the summer before, but she didn't get far enough to find it, because, as she was just making her way through the sounds, she got stuck at an answer that she later brought home, in place of the guitar chord, feeling with absolute certainty that if she didn't find the question it referred to her brain would burst. She spent the next thirteen months interrogating dozens of people, with the sole, furious intention of finding that question. Meanwhile the answer, lying in her mind, seethed with splendor and mystery. In the fourteenth month she began to write poetry, in the sixteenth her brain exploded. Destroyed by grief, her father wanted to understand what had defeated her in that way. He found it curious that a girl so intelligent could let herself be beaten by the disappearance of a question rather than by the harshness of an answer. Since he was a man of great practicality and excellent common sense, he overcame his grief, went to Modesto, and asked if he had ever heard that answer.

Of course, said Modesto.

Do you remember the question, too? the count insisted.

Naturally, said Modesto.

In fact he didn't remember a damn thing, but he was a sensible man, he had read many books, and he sincerely wanted to help that father.

How long must I wait to know the reasons for your happiness and the purpose of your despair?

The count thanked him, handed him a moderate tip, and returned home to report. His daughter greeted the sought-after question with apparent calm. The next day she retired to a convent in the neighborhood of Basilea. (She must have written the singular *Handbook for Young Girls Asleep*, which had so much success, you know, in the years before the war. Published under a nom de plume—Hérodiade—it suggested daily spiritual exercises for young women who lacked appropriate intellectual guides or any moral vigor. As far as I remember, it set out daily precepts of a curious nature but easy execution. Things like eating only yellow foods, running instead of walking, always saying yes, talking to animals, sleeping naked, pretending to be pregnant, moving in slow motion, drinking every three minutes, putting on someone else's shoes, thinking out loud, shaving one's head, acting like a Friulian hen. It was hoped that each exercise would last twelve hours. The author intended those singular tasks to produce, in girls, the capacity for self-discipline and the pleasure of acquiring a certain independence of thought. I don't know if the results were equal to the expectations. I recall distinctly, however, that, shortly after becoming successful, the author gave birth to twins whom she called First and Second, stating that she had had them through the intercession of the Archangel Michael. (Obviously, pages like these, to the editor who in a few months will be dealing with them, will seem completely useless and sadly unhelpful to the progress of the story. With the usual politeness, he will suggest that I delete them. I already know that I won't, but as of now I can admit to being no more likely than he to be right. The fact is that some write books, others read them: God knows who is in the better position to understand something about them. Is the heart of a land given to those who see it for the first time with adult wonder or to those who are born there? No one knows. Everything I've learned, in that regard, can be summed up in a few lines. One writes as one would make love to a woman, but on a night with no light, in the most absolute darkness, and so without ever seeing her. Then, the next evening, those who happen by first will take her out to dinner, or dancing, or to the races, but understanding immediately that they won't even be able to touch her, much less take her to bed. Each one lacks a piece, and rarely is the spell disclosed. When in doubt, I tend to rely on my blindness and take at face value the memory of my skin. So now I will close four parentheses, and do so with tranquil confidence, lulled by this regional train that is carrying me south.)))) Voilà.

It goes without saying that, in that flurry of activity, attention to the English deliveries diminished, and, for their part, they had become less and less frequent, in a decline that no one, honestly, had known how to interpret. A pint of Irish beer arrived, it's true, but deliveries were erratic, since they then had to wait a good seven days for another package, of limited dimensions and questionable contents: when it was opened, a book was found, and a used book, besides. The majority barely noted its arrival and immediately forgot about it, but the young Bride didn't forget it, and without appearing to do so was able to retrieve it and keep it for herself, secretly. It wasn't just any book; it was *Don Quixote*.

For several days she kept it hidden in her room and her thoughts. Repeatedly she asked herself if, by reading it as a message meant for her, she didn't risk overestimating a joke of chance. With close attention she listened to her own heart. Then she asked the Father for a meeting and, having obtained it, appeared in his study at seven in the evening, when the tasks of the day were over and the traditional evening scramble was about to begin. She had dressed with care. She spoke meekly, but remained standing and uttered every word with great assurance. She asked permission not to go on the vacation, and to stay in the House, to wait. I'm sure, she said, that the Son is about to return.

The Father looked up from some papers he was putting in order and stared at her, surprised.

You want to stay alone in the house? he asked.

Yes.

The Father smiled.

No one stays in this house when we go on vacation, he said serenely.

Since the young Bride didn't move, the Father considered it necessary to resort to conclusive reasoning.

Not even Modesto stays in the house when we go on vacation, he said.

It was, objectively, an unassailable argument, and yet the young Bride didn't seem especially impressed.

It's that the Son is about to return, she said.

Really?

I think so.

How do you know?

I don't know. I feel it.

Feeling isn't much, my dear.

But sometimes it's everything, sir.

The Father looked at her. It wasn't the first time he'd seen that meek impudence in her, and he couldn't help being fascinated by it every time. It was an inconvenient trait, but he sensed in it the promise of a patient force that would be capable of living, head held high, any life. For that reason, as he looked at the young Bride, proud in her convictions, it seemed to him for a moment that it might be a good idea to tell her everything: to warn her that the Son had disappeared and to confess to her that he had no idea of how to resolve things.

Then a suspicion that came from nowhere stopped him: that where his rational approach to the problem had failed, that girl's boundless intensity might be successful. In a moment of strange lucidity, he thought the Son might really return if only he allowed the girl to *truly* wait for him.

No one has ever stayed in this house when we go on vacation, he repeated, more to himself than to the young Bride.

Is it so important?

I think so.

Why?

In the repetition of actions we stop the world: it's like holding a child by the hand, so that he doesn't get lost.

Maybe he won't get lost. Maybe he just starts running a little, and is happy.

I wouldn't delude myself too much.

And then, after all, sooner or later he'll get lost, don't you think?

The Father thought of the Son, of the countless times he had held him by the hand.

Maybe, he said.

Why don't you trust me?

Because you are eighteen years old, signorina.

And so?

You still have a lot to learn, before you can think you're right.

You're joking, right?

I'm very serious.

You were twenty when you took a wife and a child that you didn't choose. Did someone tell you that you weren't old enough to do it?

The Father, caught off guard, made a vague gesture in the air.

That's another story, he said.

You think so?

The Father made another indecipherable gesture.

No, you don't think so, said the young Bride. You know that we are all immersed in a single story, which began a long time ago and isn't over yet.

Please sit down, signorina, it distresses me to see you standing there.

And he brought a hand to his heart.

The young Bride sat down facing him. She sought in herself a very calm, very sweet voice.

You don't think I can manage, by myself, in this house. But you have no idea how big and isolated that house in Argentina was. They left me there, for days. I wasn't afraid then, I couldn't be now, believe me. I'm only a girl, but I've crossed the ocean twice, and once I did it alone, to come here, knowing that, in doing it, I would kill my father. I seem like a girl, but I haven't been for a long time.

I know, said the Father.

Trust me.

That isn't the problem.

What is it, then?

I'm not used to trusting in the efficacy of the irrational.

I beg your pardon?

You want to stay here because you *feel* that the Son will arrive, right?

Yes.

I'm not used to making decisions on the basis of what one *feels*.

Maybe I didn't choose the right word.

Choose a better one.

I know it. I *know* that he'll return.

On the basis of what?

You think you know the Son?

The little that we're allowed to know our children. They are submerged continents, we see merely what is on the surface of the water.

But for me he's not a son, he's the man I love. Can you admit that I might know something more about him? I don't say *feel*, I say *know*.

It's possible.

Isn't that enough?

Like a flash, the suspicion that, if he just allowed that girl to *truly* wait for him, the Son would come back, returned to the Father.

He closed his eyes, and, resting his elbows on the desk, brought the palms of his hands to his face. He ran his fingertips over the wrinkles on his forehead. He remained like that for a long time. The young Bride said nothing: she waited. She was wondering what she could add, to bend that man's will. For a second she thought of talking to him about *Don Quixote*, but immediately realized that it would only complicate things. There was nothing else she could say, and now the only thing to do was wait.

The Father took his hands away from his face and settled himself placidly in the chair, leaning against the back.

As they certainly must have told you that day, in the city, he said, for years I've been grappling with a task that I chose and that, over time, I've learned to love. I'm striving to put the world in order, so to speak. I don't mean the entire world, obviously, I mean that small portion of the world that has been assigned to me.

He spoke with great tranquility, but searching for the words, one by one.

It's not an easy task, he said.

He took a letter opener from the desk, and began to twirl it in his fingers.

Lately I've been convinced that I will be able to complete this task only by making a gesture most of whose details will, unfortunately, not be under my control.

He looked up at the young Bride.

It's a gesture that has to do with dying, he said.

The young Bride didn't move a muscle.

So I often ask myself if I will be up to it, the Father continued. I have to keep in mind the fact that, for reasons I wouldn't know how to give a convincing explanation for, I find myself confronting this, like other tests, in complete solitude, or at least without the safe presence of some suitable person near me. It's a thing that can happen.

The young Bride nodded assent.

For this reason I'm wondering if it would not be too audacious, on my part, to go so far as to ask you a favor.

The young Bride raised her chin very slightly, without changing her gaze.

The Father put the letter opener on the table.

That day, when I find myself confronted by the need to make that gesture, would you be so kind as to be with me?

He said it coldly, as he might have pronounced the price of a fabric.

It's also possible, he added, that when that day arrives you won't be in this house, and in fact it's reasonable to think that I will have long since become accustomed to not to hearing about you. Yet I will know how to find you, and will send for you. I won't ask you anything in particular, it will be sufficient to have you near and to talk to you, to hear you speak. I know that I'll be in a hurry or have too much time ahead, on that day: will you promise to help me spend those hours, or those minutes, in the right way?

The young Bride laughed.

You're proposing a trade, she said.

Yes.

You'll leave me alone, in this house, if I promise to come to you, that day.

Exactly.

The young Bride laughed again, then she thought of something and became serious again.

Why me? she asked.

I don't know. But I *feel* it's right that way.

Then the young Bride shook her head, amused, and recalled that no one shuffles the cards better than a cardsharp.

All right, she said.

The Father made a slight bow.

All right, the young Bride repeated.

Yes, said the Father.

Then he got up, walked around the desk, went to the door, and before opening it turned.

Modesto won't appreciate it, he said.

He can stay, too, I'm sure he'd be happy to.

No, that's out of the question. If you want to stay, you'll stay alone.

All right.

Do you have a vague idea of what you'll do in all that time?

Of course. I'll wait for the Son.

Obviously, I'm sorry.

He stood there, without really knowing why. He had placed his hand on the doorknob, but he was still standing there.

Don't be afraid, he'll come back, said the young Bride.

By tradition they left in two honking cars. Nothing especially elegant, but the solemnity of the occasion required a certain display of grandeur. Habitually, Modesto said goodbye standing on the threshold of the entrance, even though he was ready to leave himself, his suitcase placed on the ground next to him: like any captain, he considered it his duty to be the last to abandon ship. That year, he found beside him the young Bride, and this because of the variation that the Father had announced concisely, at one of the last breakfasts, and that he had greeted without enthusiasm. The fact that it seemed to be the prelude to the return of the Son had helped him endure his irritation at the news.

So they stood on the threshold, stiffly, he and the young Bride, when the two cars set off, pistons sputtering, hands waving, and various cries. They were two fine automobiles, cream-colored. They went ten meters and stopped. They shifted into reverse and in a rather elaborate way backed up. The Mother jumped out with surprising agility and ran to the house. As she passed Modesto and the young Bride she hurriedly murmured three words.

I forgot something.

Then she disappeared into the house. She came out a few minutes later and, without even saying goodbye, ran to the cars and got in. She appeared visibly relieved.

So the cars set off again, sputtering as they had the first time, and even more animated by final waves and cheerful voices. They went ten meters and stopped. They had to shift into reverse again. This time the Mother got out with a hint of anxiety. She covered with decisive steps the distance that divided her from the entrance and disappeared into the house murmuring four words.

I forgot something else.

The young Bride turned toward Modesto, giving him a questioning gaze.

Modesto cleared his throat with two precise contractions of the larynx, one short, the other long. The young Bride's education in that cuneiform writing wasn't so advanced, but she sensed vaguely that it was all under control, and was calm.

The Mother got back in the car, the engines revved again, and in a bubble of noisy joy goodbyes were said conclusively and without regret. This time, before stopping, they traveled some meters farther. They shifted into reverse with a certain fluidity, since they had learned how.

The Mother returned to the house humming, with the most complete self-control. She seemed to know what she wanted. When she reached the doorway, however, right next to

Modesto and the young Bride, she was seized by some second thoughts. She stopped. She seemed to be focusing on some belated reflection. She shrugged and said three words.

But no, O.K.

Then she turned around and went back to the cars, still humming.

How many times does she do it? asked the young Bride in a serious tone.

Usually four, answered Modesto, imperturbable.

So it wasn't a surprise to see the cars leave, stop after a certain distance, back up, and spit out the Mother, who this time walked up the path to the house, apparently furious, her steps heavy, cursing softly in an uninterrupted litany of which the young Bride caught, as she passed, an indefinite fragment.

Let them all go to hell.

Or maybe "yell," it was hard to tell.

The Mother re-emerged from the house, after an absence longer than the previous ones, clutching in her hand a piece of silverware, and waving it in the air. She seemed no less furious than before. As she passed, the young Bride discerned that the litany had veered toward French. She seemed to recognize distinctly the word *connard*.

But it could also be *moutarde*, it was hard to tell.

Since Modesto raised an arm to wave, the young Bride understood that the ceremony was concluding and so she, too, with sincere happiness, and perhaps a tinge of regret, began to say goodbye, standing on tiptoe and waving her hand in the air. She saw them growing distant, in a cloud of dust and emotion, and for a moment she was gripped by the fear that she had demanded too much from herself. Then she saw the two cars stop.

Oh no, she let escape.

But this time they didn't back up, and it wasn't the Mother who jumped down off the running board. Amid the dust they saw the Daughter running toward the house, with her crooked gait, but heedless and decisive, even beautiful in her vaguely childish hurry. She stopped in front of the young Bride.

You won't run away, right? she asked in a firm voice.

But her eyes were tearing, and it wasn't because of the dust.

I'm not even thinking of it, said the young Bride, surprised.

Here, let's make it so you won't run away.

Then she went up to the young Bride and embraced her.

They remained like that, for a few moments.

The Daughter, returning to the car, was no longer in a hurry. She walked with her sad, dragging gait, but she was serene. She got in without turning around again.

Then they all disappeared around the first bend, and this time they had really left.

Modesto let the snorting of the two automobiles disappear in the distance of the countryside, then, in the regular silence of nothing, heaved a faint sigh and picked up his suitcase.

I've left you three books, hidden in the bathroom. Three texts of a certain notoriety.

Really?

As I told you, the pantry is full of food—be content with cold meals and don't touch the wine cellar, except in case of absolute necessity.

The young Bride had trouble imagining what a case of absolute necessity might be.

I'll leave you my address, in the city, but I wouldn't want you to misunderstand. I'm leaving it only because, if the Son really should arrive, he might need me.

The young Bride took the piece of paper, folded in two, that he was handing her.

I think that's everything, Modesto concluded.

He decided that at that precise moment he was starting his vacation, so he went off without taking the first steps backward, as his most glorious number would have required. He confined himself to a very slight bow.

The young Bride let him go a few steps, then she called to him.

Modesto.

Yes?

Isn't it a burden to have to always be so perfect?

No, in fact. It releases me from seeking other purposes for my actions.

What do you mean?

I don't have to ask myself every day why I live.

Ah.

It's comforting.

I imagine.

Do you have other questions?

Yes, one.

Tell me.

What do you do when they leave and close the house?

I get drunk, Modesto answered with unpredictable readiness and heedless sincerity.

For two weeks?

Yes, every day for two weeks.

And where?

I have a person who takes care of me, in the city.

May I go so far as to ask what type of person it is?

A likable man. The man I've loved all my life.

Ah.

He has a family. But it's arranged so that in those two weeks he comes to stay with me.

Very practical.

Rather.

So you won't be alone, in the city.

No.

I'm happy for that.

Thank you.

They looked at each other in silence.

No one knows, said Modesto.

Evidently, said the young Bride.

Then she waved, even though she would have liked to embrace him, or even kiss him lightly, or something like that.

He understood, and was grateful for her composure.

He walked away slowly, slightly bent, immediately distant.

The young Bride went into the house and closed the door behind her.

It was a torrid summer, that year. Horizons vaporized tremulous dreams. Clothes stuck to the skin. Animals dragged themselves along insensibly. It was hard to breathe.

It was even worse in the house, which the young Bride kept closed up, with the idea of letting it seem deserted. The air stagnated lazily, sleeping in a kind of damp lethargy. Even the flies—usually capable, it should be noted, of inexplicable optimism—seemed unconvinced. But to the young Bride it didn't matter. In a certain sense, she liked moving slowly, her skin shining with sweat, her feet seeking the comfort of stone. Since no one could see her, she often went through the rooms naked, discovering strange sensations. She didn't sleep in her bed, but around the house. It occurred to her to use the places where she had seen the Uncle sleeping, and so she inhabited them one after the other, in sleep. When she slept in these places naked, she felt a pleasant agitation. She had no schedule, because she had decided to let the pace of the days be dictated by the urgency of her desires and the pristine geometry of her needs. So she slept when she was sleepy, she ate when she was hungry. But don't think that it made her wild. For all those days she took meticulous care of herself—after all, she was waiting for a man. She brushed her hair repeatedly, she spent long moments at the mirror, she stayed in the water for hours. Once a day she dressed with the utmost elegance, in the Daughter's or the Mother's clothes, and in her splendor she sat in the big room, reading. Occasionally she felt oppressed by the solitude, or by an uncontrollable anguish, and then she chose a corner of the house where she recalled having seen or experienced something noteworthy. She would crouch down, open her legs, and caress herself. As if by magic, everything resettled itself. It was a strange sensation to touch herself on the chair in which the Father had asked to die with her. It was also remarkable to do it on the marble floor of the chapel. When she was hungry she got something from the pantry and then went to sit at the big table for breakfasts. As noted, it was traditional to leave twenty-five places, flawlessly set, as if at any moment a horde of guests were to arrive. The young Bride decided that each time she would eat at one of those places. When she finished eating, she took everything away, washed, cleaned, and left the place at the table empty, the place setting gone. So her meals were like a slow hemorrhage through which the table lost meaning and purpose, progressively emptied of every jewel and any ornament: the blinding white of the table-cloth advanced, naked.

Once, having inadvertently fallen asleep, she was wakened by the sudden certainty that waiting for a man, alone, in that house, was a tragically vain and ridiculous act. She was sleeping, naked, on a carpet she had unrolled in front of the door of the living room. She looked for something to cover herself with, because she felt cold. She pulled a sheet that was covering a nearby chair over herself. Mistakenly, she went back over her life in her mind, to find something that would break that strange, sudden fall into emptiness. All she did was make things worse. Everything seemed to her wrong or horrible. The Family was crazy, her trip to the brothel grotesque, any phrase uttered with a straight back absurd, Modesto cloying, the Father mad, the Mother ill, those places ignoble, her father's end disgusting, the fate of her brothers desperate, her youth wasted. With a lucidity one has only in dreams, she understood that she no longer possessed anything, that she wasn't beautiful enough to save herself, that she had killed her father, and that, little by little, the Family was robbing her of her innocence.

Is it possible that it has to end like that? she asked, frightened.

I'm only eighteen, she thought, with fear.

So, in order not to die, she took refuge where she knew she would find the last line of resistance to disaster. She forced herself to think about the Son. But *think* is a reductive word to define an operation that she knew was quite complex. Three years of silence and separation were not easy to retrace. So much distance had accumulated that the Son had long since stopped being, for the young Bride, an easily accessible thought, or memory, or sentiment. He had become *a place*. An enclave, buried in the landscape of her feelings, which she couldn't always find again. Often she set off to reach it, but got lost on the way. It would have been simpler for her if she could have had available some physical desire to hold onto, in order to scale the walls of oblivion. But desire for the Son—his mouth, his hands, his skin—was something it wasn't simple to return to. She could distinctly summon to memory particular instants in which she had desired him even in a devastating way, but now, staring at them, it seemed to her that she was staring at a room in which, in place of colors, little pieces of paper were stuck to the walls with the names of the hues written on them: indigo, Venetian red, sand yellow. Turquoise. It wasn't pleasant to admit, but it was so. And even more, now that circumstances had led her to know other pleasures, with other people, with other bodies: they weren't enough to erase the memory of the Son, but certainly they had placed him in a sort of prehistory in which everything seemed mythical as well as inexorably literary. For that reason, following the traces of physical desire wasn't often, for the young Bride, the best system for finding the road that led to the hiding place of her love. Occasionally, she preferred to dig out of her memory the beauty of certain phrases, or certain gestures—a beauty of which the Son was a master. She found this beauty intact, then, in memory. And for a moment this seemed to restore to her the spell of the Son and bring her back to the exact point at which her journey aimed. But it was an illusion more than anything. She found herself contemplating marvelous objects that still lay in the cabinets of distance, impossible to touch, inaccessible to the heart. So the agonizing sense of ultimate loss was mixed with the pleasure of admiration, and the Son grew even more distant, almost unapproachable, now. In order not to truly lose him, the young Bride had had to learn that in reality no quality of the Son—or detail, or marvel—was now sufficient to enable her to cross the abyss of distance, because no man, however loved, is enough by himself to defeat the destructive power of absence. What the young Bride understood was that only by thinking of the two of them, together, was she able to sink into herself to where the permanence of her love dwelt, intact. She went back then to certain states of mind, certain ways of perceiving, which she still remembered very well. She thought of the two of them, together, and could feel a certain heat, or the tone of certain nuances, even the quality of a certain silence. A particular light. Then it was given to her to find what she sought, in the definite sensation that a place existed to which the world was not admitted, and which coincided with the perimeter marked by their two bodies, kindled by their being together, and made unassailable by their anomaly. If she could reach that sensation, everything became harmless again. Since the disaster of every life around her, and even of her own, was no longer a danger to her happiness but, if anything, the counterpart that made still more necessary and invincible the refuge that she and the Son had created, loving each other. They were the demonstration of a theorem that refuted the world, and when she could return to that conviction, all fear abandoned her and a new, sweet confidence took possession of her. There was nothing more wonderful in the world.

As she lay on the carpet, curled up under that dusty sheet, this was the journey the young Bride made, saving her life.

So she still had her love entirely available when, two days later, at a table where nine settings remained, and just as she was preparing for another to vanish, she heard in the distance the sound of an automobile, dim at first and then increasingly clear—she heard it arrive at the house, stop, and finally turn off. She got up, left everything as it was on the table, and went to her room to prepare. She had long since chosen a dress for the occasion. She put it on. She brushed her hair and thought that the Son had never seen her so beautiful. She wasn't afraid, she wasn't nervous, she didn't have questions. She heard the engine of the automobile start up again and then grow faint. Barefoot, she went down the stairs and through the house, her steps firm. When she reached the front door she broadened her shoulders, as the Mother had taught her. Then she opened the door and went out.

In the courtyard she saw a number of trunks, resting on the ground. She knew them. Sitting on the biggest—a large creature of dark leather, slightly scratched on one side—she saw the Uncle, dressed just as he had been when he left, and motionless. He was sleeping. The young Bride approached.

Did something happen?

Since the Uncle continued to sleep, she sat down next to him. She realized that he was sleeping with his eyes half open, and that occasionally he trembled. She touched his forehead. It was burning.

You're not well, said the young Bride.

The Uncle opened his eyes and looked at her as if he were seeking to understand something.

It's lucky to find you here, signorina, he said.

The young Bride shook her head.

You're not well.

No, I'm not, said the Uncle. Would you mind very much doing a couple of things for me? he asked.

No, said the young Bride.

Then be so kind as to fill the tub with very hot water. Then would you open the yellow trunk, the small one, and find a sealed bottle, in it there's some white powder. Take it.

It was a long sentence, and it must have tired him, because he sank back into sleep.

The Young Bride didn't move. She thought of herself, of the Son, and of life.

When it seemed to her that the Uncle was about to wake, she got up.

I'm going to find a doctor, she said.

No, please, don't, it's not necessary. I know what it is.

There was a long pause and a nap.

That is, I don't know what it is, but I know how to treat it. A hot bath and that white powder will be enough, believe me. Naturally it will do me good to sleep a little.

He did for three days, almost without interruption. He stationed himself in the second-floor hall, the one with the seven windows. He lay on the stone floor, his head resting on a shirt folded in four. He didn't eat, he seldom drank. At regular intervals the young Bride went up and set beside him a glass in which she had dissolved the white powder: each time, she found him at a different point in the hall, sometimes curled up in a corner, other times lying under a window, composed, tranquil, but trembling: she imagined him crawling on the stone, like an animal whose paws had been crushed. Every so often she stopped to look at him, without saying anything. Under a suit dripping with sweat, she sensed a body that seemed to be all ages, scattered in the details, without a precise plan: the hands of a boy, the legs of an old man. Once she ran her fingers through his sodden hair. He didn't move. Surprised, she was aware that she was thinking, without the least distress, that that man was perhaps dying: nothing seemed to her more inappropriate than to try to stop him. She went back downstairs and began waiting for the son again, with what seemed to her the same intensity and the same beauty as before. But that night, when she returned to the Uncle, he clutched her wrist, with strange energy, and, sleeping, told her that he was tremendously mortified.

For what? the young Bride asked.

I've ruined everything for you, he said.

And the young Bride understood that it was true. First the surprise, then the instinct to make herself useful, had kept her from realizing that the Uncle's arrival had marred something perfect, and diverted a flight that was gliding along without errors. She saw again all her magnificent gestures, which she hadn't stopped performing, and understood that since the arrival of that man they had been done without happiness and without faith. I've stopped waiting, she said to herself.

She went back down without saying a word, and walked through the rooms, furious at first, then desolate. She stared at the door for a long time, until she understood with inexorable lucidity that it had opened to let in the wrong man, at the wrong moment, for the wrong reasons. She went so far as to think that, in some mysterious way, the Son must have realized it, while he was traveling on the road that would take him home: she saw him at the moment when he set a suitcase down on the ground, let a train leave without getting on, stopped a car and turned off the engine. No, please, no, she said to him. Please, she said to herself.

When the Uncle came downstairs after six days, perfectly shaved and rather elegant in a tobacco-colored suit, he found her sitting on the floor, in a corner, her face unrecognizable.

He looked at her just for an instant before heading to the kitchen, where he fell asleep. He hadn't eaten for a long time: finally he did, with a certain moderation, still sleeping. Then he went to the cellar, and disappeared there for two or three hours: the time required for him to choose a bottle of champagne and one of red wine. He returned to the kitchen, where he put the champagne on ice. Without resting even for a moment, he uncorked the bottle of wine and let it breathe on the table. Worn out by his labors he dragged himself to the dining room and dropped into a chair, just in front of the young Bride. He slept for ten minutes, then opened his eyes.

Tomorrow they return, he said.

The young Bride nodded. She might also mean that nothing mattered to her.

I wonder if you have any engagements for this evening, continued the Uncle.

The young Bride said nothing. She didn't move.

I take it as a no, the Uncle informed her. In that case, I would be honored to invite you to dinner, if it would not cause you uneasiness or, indeed, distress.

Then he fell asleep.

The young Bride stared at him. She wondered if she hated him. Yes, of course, she hated him: but no more than she hated everyone. It seemed to her that neither sweetness, nor folly, nor beauty remained to her, anywhere, ever since they had all agreed to devastate her soul. Could she do anything other than hate them? If you have no future, hating is an instinct.

Where do you want to take me? she asked.

She had to wait ten minutes for an answer.

Oh, nowhere. I thought of dining here, I'll see to everything. I promise you it will be of a certain quality.

You cook?

Sometimes.

Sleeping?

The Uncle opened his eyes. He stared at the young Bride for a long time. It was something he never did. Stare at someone for a long time.

Yes, sleeping, he said, finally.

He got up, took a brief nap leaning on the plate rack, then headed toward the front door.

I think I'll take a little walk, he said.

Then, before going out, he turned to the young Bride.

I'll expect you at nine. Would you mind terribly wearing a beautiful dress?

The young Bride didn't answer.

I can still see that set table, the same as the breakfasts table, but now it had an essential elegance, with the symmetry of two places, one opposite the other, and the white of the tablecloth spreading around them. The light was right, the placement of the silverware meticulous, the alignment of the glasses perfect. An arrangement of foods that seemed to have been chosen for their colors waited on the plates. Five candles, nothing else.

The dress I had chosen was irresistible. The same in which I had lived and sweated in the previous days, ankle-length, with an ordinary neckline, dirty, very light. But underneath I had taken off everything. I wasn't worried about what could be seen from the outside; the very simple sensation that I had was enough. I was going to a dinner, naked. I hadn't washed, my hands were the same as they'd been for days, on my feet were the dust, the dirt, the smell. I had cried a thousand times, and I didn't even run water over my face. But I did something with my hair that the Mother would have liked: I brushed it all day, with perfumed brushes: in front of the mirror I gathered it on my head, trying countless architectures to find the most seductive and make the time pass. I chose a height that was slightly arrogant but in the front innocent, the whole complex enough to hint at a trick. I could let it down, in an instant, with a single skillful movement of my neck.

For all this I didn't know the reason. I was impelled by instinct, without thinking. Nothing could be more alien to me, at that moment, than ambition toward a goal, or the expectation of some result. Time had been replaced by an infinite heat, knowledge by a distracted indolence, and all my desires by a harmless, mute suffering under my heart. I have never existed so little as on that ship, which gently cleaves the boiling dampness of the evening, transporting me and my eleven things to the white of an island that knows nothing of me—and I almost nothing of it. From land we'll both be invisible, in the space of a thought—vanished to the world. But enveloped by a graceless beauty I was there at nine, in a curious homage to precision that, sincerely, I now can't understand. I heard the Uncle moving about in the kitchen, then I saw him arrive. He hadn't changed, either, he had only taken off his jacket. He arrived carrying the bottle of champagne, chilled.

The food is on the plates, he said.

He sat down at the table and fell asleep. He had barely looked at me. I began to eat—I chose the colors, one by one. He drank, in his sleep. I didn't use the silverware, I wiped my fingers on the dress. But I don't know why. Every so often, without opening his eyes, the Uncle poured me some champagne. I don't remember asking myself about the absurd precision of that gesture, or its unlikely punctuality. I drank and that was all. Besides, in that house of life interrupted, in the privacy of our mad liturgies, besieged by our poetic maladies, we were characters orphaned of any logic. I continued to eat, he slept. I wasn't uncomfortable, I liked it—precisely because it was absurd, I liked it. I began to think that it would be one of the best dinners of my life. I wasn't bored, I was myself, I drank champagne. At a certain point I started talking, but slowly, and only about foolish things. In his sleep the Uncle occasionally smiled. Or he gestured with his hand in the air. He was listening to me, in some way, and it was pleasant to talk to him. It was all very light, elusive. I wouldn't have been able to say what I was experiencing. It was a spell. I felt it closing in on us and when there was no longer anything else in the world except my voice, I sensed that in reality nothing that was happening was happening, nor would it ever happen. For a reason that must have originated in the absurd intensity of our defeats, nothing of what the two of us could do, that evening, would remain in the ledger of life. No calculation would take us into account, no sum would come out different as a result of our activity, no debt would be discharged, no credit opened. We were hidden in a fold of creation, invisible to fate and freed from any consequence. So, while I ate, sticking my fingers in the warm colors of the food that had been arranged with maniacal care, I understood with utter certainty that that lovely emptiness, without direction and without purpose, exiled from any past and incapable of any future, must be, *literally*, the spell under which that man had lived, every minute, for years. I understood that it was the world into which he had expelled himself—inaccessible, without names, parallel to ours, immutable—and I understood that that evening I had been admitted to it, thanks to my folly. It must have required a lot of courage for that man to imagine an invitation like that. Or great solitude, I thought. Now he was sleeping, in front of me, and I, for the first time, knew what he was really doing. He was translating the intolerable distance that he had chosen into a polite metaphor, legible to anyone, ironic, innocuous. For he was a kind man.

I wiped my fingers on my dress. I looked at him. He was sleeping.

How long since you haven't slept? I asked.

He opened his eyes.

For years, signorina.

Maybe he was moved, or maybe I imagined it.

What I miss more than anything else is dreams, he said.

And he remained with his eyes open, awake, looking at me. There wasn't much light, and it wasn't easy to see what color they were. Gray, maybe. With bits of gold. I had never seen them.

It's all very good, I said.

Thank you.

You should cook more often.

You think?

Wasn't there also a bottle of red wine?

You're right, I'm sorry.

He got up, and disappeared into the kitchen.

I also got up. I took my glass and went to sit on the floor, in a corner of the room.

When he returned, he came over to pour me some wine, then he stood there, not knowing what to do.

Sit here, I said.

It was an immense chair, one of those places where I had seen him sleeping countless times, while the breakfasts flowed, river-like. If I think about it carefully, it was the same chair from which he had greeted my return, with a remark I hadn't forgotten: *You must have done a lot of dancing, signorina, over there. I'm glad of it.*

Do you like to dance? I asked him.

I liked it very much, yes.

What else did you like?

Everything. Too much, perhaps.

What do you miss most?

Apart from dreams?

Apart from those.

The dreams you have in the daytime.

Did you have a lot?

Yes.

Did you fulfill them?

Yes.

And how is it?

Pointless.

I don't believe it.

In fact you mustn't believe it. It's too early to believe it, at your age.

What age am I?

A young age.

Does it make a difference?

Yes.

Explain it to me.

You'll find out, one day.

I want to know now.

It would be of no use.

Still with that story?

Which?

That it's all pointless.

I didn't say that.

You said it's useless to fulfill one's dreams.

That, yes.

Why?

For me it was pointless.

Tell me.

No.

Do it.

Signorina, I must really ask you . . .

And he closed his eyes, letting his head fall back, against the chair. It seemed drawn by an invisible force.

Ah no, I said.

I put down my glass, I got up, and stood over him, my legs spread. I found myself with my sex on his, it wasn't what I wanted. But I began to sway. I stood with my back straight, I swayed slowly over him, I placed my hands on his shoulders, I looked at him.

He opened his eyes.

Please, he repeated.

You owe me something. Your story will be enough, I said.

I don't believe I owe you anything.

Oh, yes.

Really?

You weren't the one who was supposed to return, it was the Son.

I'm sorry.

Don't think you can get out of it like that.

No?

You've ruined everything for me, now I want at least your true story in exchange.

He looked at the exact point where I was swaying.

It's a story like so many others, he said.

It doesn't matter, I want it.

I wouldn't even know where to begin.

Begin at the end. The moment you started sleeping and stopped living.

I was at a table in a Café.

Was there someone with you?

No longer.

You were alone.

Yes. I fell asleep without even nodding my head. Sleeping, I finished my pastis, and that was the first time. When I woke up and saw the empty glass, I knew it would be like that forever.

I wonder about the people around.

In what sense?

Well, the waiters, didn't they come and wake you?

It was a somewhat rundown Café, with very old waiters. At that age you understand many things.

They let you sleep.

Yes.

What time was it?

I don't know, afternoon.

How did you end up in that Café?

I told you it's a long story, I don't know if I want to tell it, and besides you're swaying against me and I don't know why.

To keep you from going back to your world.

Ah.

The story.

If I tell you will you sit on the floor again?

I wouldn't think of it, I like it. You don't like it?

I beg your pardon?

I asked if you like it.

What?

This, my legs spread, my sex rubbing against yours?

He closed his eyes, his head slid back a little, I tightened my fingers on his shoulders, he opened his eyes again, he looked at me.

There was a woman I loved very much, he said.

There was a woman I loved very much. She had a beautiful way of doing everything. There is no one in the world like her.

One day she arrived with a small book, used, the cover was a very elegant blue. The great thing was that she had crossed the city to bring it to me, she had seen it in an old bookstore, and had dropped everything to bring it to me immediately, she found it so irresistible, and precious. The book had a magnificent title: *How to Abandon Ship*. It was a handbook. The letters on the cover were clear, perfect. The illustrations inside laid out with infinite care. Can you understand that a book like that is worth more than a lot of literature?

Maybe.

You don't find at least the title irresistible?

Maybe.

It doesn't matter. What matters is that she arrived with that book. For a long time I carried it with me, I loved it so much.

It was small, it fit in my pocket. I went to teach, I put it on the desk, then I put it back in my pocket. I must have read maybe a couple of pages, it was fairly boring, but that wasn't the point. It was good to hold it in your hand, leaf through it. It was good to think that however disgusting life might be, I had that book in my pocket and next to me a woman who had given it to me. Can you understand that?

Of course, I'm not an idiot.

Ah, I forgot the best part. On the first page, which was blank, there was a rather poignant dedication. It was a used book, as I said, and on the first page there was this dedication: *To Terry after the first month of his stay in St. Thomas's Hospital. Papa and Mamma.* Your imagination can wander for days on a dedication like that. It was that type of beauty that I found heartrending. And that the woman I loved so much could understand. Why am I telling you all this? Ah, yes, the Café. Are you sure you want to go on?

Of course.

Time passed, and in that time I lost the woman I loved so much, for reasons that here don't interest us. Moreover, I'm not sure I understood them. Anyway, I continued to carry with me . . .

Wait a minute. Who said it doesn't interest us?

Me.

Speak for yourself.

No, I'm speaking for both of us, if you don't like it get down from there and have the Son tell you the story, when he arrives.

All right, all right, there's no need to . . .

So it was a strange time, for me, it seemed a little like being a widower, I walked the way widowers do, you know, a little stunned, with eyes like a bird that doesn't get it. You know what I mean?

Yes, I think so.

But always with my little book in my pocket. It was idiotic, I should have thrown away everything that the woman I loved so much had left behind, but how do you do it, it's like a shipwreck, a lot of things, of all kinds, remain floating on the surface, in these cases. You can't, really, clean up. And you have to hold on to something, when you can't swim anymore. So I had that book in my pocket, that day, at the Café, and, look, by now months had passed, since it had ended. But I had the book in my pocket. I had a date with a woman, nothing very important, she wasn't a special woman, I scarcely knew her. I liked how she dressed. She had a lovely laugh, that's it. She didn't talk much, and, there in the Café that day, she spoke so little that it all seemed to me tremendously depressing. So I pulled out that book and began to talk to her about it, telling her that I had just bought it. She found the story strange, but in some way curious, she relaxed a little, she began to ask me about myself, we started to talk, I said something that made her laugh. It was all simple, even pleasant. She seemed to me more beautiful, every so often we leaned toward each other, we forgot the people at the other tables, it was just the two of us, delightful. Then she had to go, and it seemed natural to kiss. I saw her disappear around a corner, with a very attractive walk. Then I lowered my gaze. On the table were our two glasses of pastis, half full, and the blue book. I placed a hand on the book and I was struck by its infinite neutrality. So much love and time and devotion had been deposited in it, from Terry's time to mine, and so much life, and of the best kind: and yet it was nothing, it hadn't put up the least resistance to my little infamy, hadn't rebelled, had merely sat there, available to any other adventure, utterly without a permanent meaning, light and empty as an object that had been born right then, rather than one that had grown up in the heart of so many lives. So I came to understand our defeat, in all its tragic import, and I felt vanquished by an unspeakable and final weariness. Maybe I realized that something had broken, forever, inside me. I felt that I was slipping some distance away from things, and that I would never be able to retrace that path. I let myself go. It was splendid. I felt any anguish dissolve, and disappear. I found myself in a luminous serenity, lightly veined with sadness, and I recognized the land that I had always sought. The people around saw that I was sleeping. That's the whole story.

You can't think I'll believe that you've been sleeping for years because of a silly thing like that . . .

It was only the last in an impressive series of silly things like that.

Like?

The treachery of things. You know what I'm talking about?

No.

It's very instructive: to see how objects contain nothing of the meaning we give them. All it takes is an oblique circumstance, a tiny adjustment to the trajectory, and in an instant they are part of a completely different story. Do you think that this chair will be different for having listened to my words or having held your body and mine? Maybe, months from now, someone will *die* in this chair, and, no matter what we do tonight that is unforgettable, it will accommodate that death and that's it. It will do it as well as possible, and as if it had been constructed for that purpose. Nor will it react when, maybe just an hour later, someone will drop into it, and laugh at a vulgar joke, or tell a story in which the dead man plays the role of the perfect idiot. You see it, the infinite neutrality?

Is it so important?

Of course. In the behavior of objects one learns a phenomenon that is to some extent true for everything. Believe me, it's the same for places, people, even feelings, ideas, too.

What is it?

We have an incredible force with which we give meaning to things, to places, to everything: and yet we can't secure anything, it all goes back to neutral right away—borrowed objects, fleeting ideas, feelings as fragile as crystal. Even bodies, the desire of bodies: unpredictable. We can bombard any piece of the world with all the intensity we're capable of and, an hour later, it's newly reborn. You can understand something, know it thoroughly, and it has already shifted, it knows nothing of you, it has its own mysterious life, which takes no account of what you've made of it. Those who love us betray us, and we betray those we love. We can't secure anything, believe me. When I was young, trying to explain to myself the mute sorrow that clung to me, I was convinced that the problem lay in my incapacity to find my path: but you see, in reality we walk a lot, with courage, intuition, passion, each of us on our own just path, without errors. But we leave no traces. I don't know why. Our footsteps leave no imprint. Maybe we are astute, swift, mean animals, but incapable of marking the earth. I don't know. But, believe me, we don't leave traces even in ourselves. Thus there is nothing that survives our intention, and what we construct is never built.

You really believe that?

Yes.

Maybe it's something that concerns only you.

I don't think so.

It concerns me, too?

I imagine so, yes.

In what way?

In many ways.

Tell me one.

Those who love us betray us, and we betray those we love.

What do I have to do with that?

It's what's happening to you.

I'm not betraying anyone.

No? What do you call this?

This what?

You know very well.

This has nothing to do with it.

Precisely. It has nothing to do with your great love, it has nothing to do with the Son, it has nothing to do with the idea you have of yourself. There is no trace of all that in the actions you are performing at this moment. Doesn't it seem odd to you? No trace.

I stayed here to wait for him, doesn't that mean something?

I don't know. You tell me.

I never stopped loving him, I'm here for him, and he's always with me.

You're convinced of it?

Of course. We never stopped being together.

Yet I don't see him here.

He's coming.

It's what they all believe.

And so?

Maybe the truth would interest you.

The truth is that the Son is arriving.

I'm afraid not, signorina.

What do you know about it?

I know that the last time they saw him was a year ago. He was embarking on a cutter, a small sailboat. Since then no one has heard anything about him.

What the hell are you talking about?

Naturally it wasn't something that could be communicated to the Father, so crudely, and abruptly. So we preferred first to put it off and then to manage it in a, let's say, more gradual manner. It couldn't be ruled out, moreover, that the Son would reappear out of nothing, one day or other. You've stopped swaying, signorina.

But you haven't.

I no, it's true.

Why are you telling me these lies? Do you want to hurt me?

I don't know.

Are they lies?

No.

Tell me the truth.

It's the truth: the Son disappeared.

When?

A year ago.

And who told you?

It was Comandini who took care of things.

Him.

He was the only one who knew, until a few days ago. Then he came to tell me, shortly before we left. He wanted some advice.

And all that stuff?

The two rams and the rest?

Yes.

Well, the affair became complicated when you arrived. It was hard to keep dragging things out. So to Comandini it seemed that a very lengthy, endless relocation could gain some time.

Comandini sent those things?

Yes.

I can't believe it.

It was a form of courtesy toward the Father.

Nonsense . . .

I'm sorry, signorina.

I will hate you all, with all my soul, forever, until the day the Son returns.

The Uncle closed his eyes, I felt his shoulders under my hands change their weight.

I tightened my grip.

Don't do it, I said. Don't go.

He reopened his eyes, his gaze empty.

Now let me go, signorina, please.

I won't even think of it.

Please.

I won't stay here alone.

Please.

He closed his eyes again, he was leaving, to return to his spell.

Did you hear me? I won't stay here alone.

I have to go, really.

He was already talking in his sleep.

So I tightened one hand around his throat. He opened his eyes, astonished. I stared at him, and this time it was a firm look, maybe mean.

Where the hell do you think you're going? I said.

The Uncle looked around, more than anything to avoid my eyes. Or to look for an answer, in things.

I won't stay here alone, I said. You come away with me.

I saw his eyelids descend, while he drew a long breath. But I knew that I wouldn't let him go. I could still feel his sex, under mine, I hadn't stopped dancing for a moment. I took my dress off, over my head, with a movement that couldn't frighten him. He opened his eyes again and looked at me. I took my hands off his shoulders and began to unbutton his shirt, because the Mother had taught me that it was my right. I didn't lean over to kiss him, I didn't caress him, ever. With a single movement of my neck, in an instant, I loosened my hair. I got down to the last button of the shirt and I didn't stop there. I kept my gaze on the Uncle's eyes, I wouldn't let him return to his spell. He looked at my hands, then he looked into my eyes, then he looked at my hands again. He didn't seem to be afraid, or to have questions, or curiosity. I took his sex in my hand and for a while I held it firmly, tight in my palm, like something that I had returned from a distance to retrieve. I moved my spread legs forward, and I remembered my grand-mother's lovely expression: a skillful belly. I was about to understand its meaning.

Don't do it with hatred, said the Uncle.

I came down on him and took him inside me.

I don't do it out of love, I said—and I remember all the rest but I'll keep it for myself, about that strange night, spent in a crack in the world, not to be found in the ledger of the living, stolen for hours from defeat, and given back at dawn, when the first light filtered through the blind, and I, holding that man in my arms, let him fall asleep, this time for real, and restored him to his dreams.

It was late when we awoke. We looked at each other and understood that we should not be found like that. The instinct to start over, always. We began to put things in order, hurriedly, I changed, he went to his room. He moved as I had never seen him, lining up his gestures with confidence, eyes vivid, steps graceful. It occurred to me that it would be easy, for the Daughter, to love him.

We didn't say a word. Only, at a certain point, I asked him:

And now what will you do?

And you? he answered.

In the noonday sun someone knocked at the door, respectful but firm.

Modesto.

It's more or less at this point that I left my computer on the seat of a bus. A bus that crossed the island from north to south, gliding along roads scarcely wider than itself, with foolish precision. At a certain point I got off and left the computer on the seat. When I realized it, the bus had already disappeared. It was a nice computer, apart from everything else. Inside was my book.

Naturally it wouldn't have been difficult to get it back, but the truth is that I let it go. To understand you have to take into account the light, the sea, the dogs moving slowly in the sun, how the people live there. The South of the world suggests curious priorities. There is a particular approach to prob- lems—solving them isn't the first thing that comes to mind. So I walked a while, I sat on a wall, at the port, and then I began watching the boats come and go. I like that whatever they do, they do it slowly. If you look at them from a distance, I mean. It's a kind of dance, it seems to involve some form of wisdom, or solemnity. There is also some disenchantment at times. Maybe a hint of renunciation—gentle. It's the marvel of ports.

So I stayed there, and things went well.

Then, at night, I returned to the business of the computer, but without particular anxieties, or fears. It may seem strange, since writing on that computer, and constructing my book, was for months the only activity I could carry out with sufficient passion and constant attention. I should have shit myself out of fear, that's what I should have done. Instead I thought, very simply, that I would continue to write, and that I would do it in my mind. It seemed to me in fact a natural, and inevitable, epilogue. Fingers on the keyboard suddenly seemed to me use- lessly harsh, or an intricate appendix to a gesture that could be much lighter, and more elusive. Besides, for a long time I'd been writing my book walking, or lying on the floor, or at night in the darkness of my insomnia: and with the computer, I tight- ened its screws, polished it with wax, packed it carefully—all that repertory of craftsmanlike attentions whose exact pur- pose, to be sincere, I now no longer remember. Surely there must have been one. But I've forgotten it. Maybe it wasn't so important.

Further, one has to consider that, if you are born to do it, writing is an act that coincides with memory: what you write, you recall. So it would be inaccurate to state that I had lost my book, since, to tell the truth, I could recite it all aloud, or, if not all, let's say at least the parts that counted for something. At most I could not remember certain sentences exactly: but it should also be said that, in bringing them back to the surface, from the place where they had drifted, I ended up rewriting them, in my mind, in a form very close to the original but not identical, the result being a sort of blurring, or echo, or doubling, in which what I imagined I had written developed, splendidly. For, in the end, the only phrase that can accurately translate a writer's particular intention is never just a sentence but the stratified sum of all the sentences he imagined before, then wrote, then remembered: they should be piled up, one on top of the other, transparent, and perceived simultaneously, like a chord. It's what memory does, in its visionary imprecision. So, to be objective, I had not only not lost my book but in a certain sense had found it again in its entirety, now that it had dematerialized, retreating into the winter quarters of my mind. I could summon it to the surface at any moment with a barely perceptible effort, situated in some recess of my body that I didn't know how to describe: it reappeared in a fleeting splendor compared with which the clear orderliness of a printed page displayed the rigidity of a tombstone.

Or at least so it seemed to me, sitting there in a trattoria at the port, that evening, on the island. I'm a genius at making things that went badly go well. I could find advantages even in being stuck in an elevator on Christmas Day. It's a trick I learned from my father (ah, he's still alive and he still plays at night on his personal, nine-hole golf course). To have something to relate at lunch the next day, for example.

I thought of these things, and meanwhile I reread some of the book, here and there I rewrote it, all in my head: while mechanically I dipped the bread in the meatball sauce.

At some point a fat, cheerful fellow sitting at a nearby table, also alone, asked me if everything was going well. I thought I must have done something strange—it was possible, when I'm reading and writing the book in my head I don't control the other parts of my body very well. Those which the book hasn't entered, I mean. The ankles, maybe.

I came out of my book and told him that everything was going very well.

I was writing, I told him.

He nodded yes with his head, as if it were a thing that used to happen to him, too, all the time, years ago, when he was still young.

Now he was in his sixties.

Placid and self-satisfied, he wanted to inform me of the fact that he was there, at the seaside, because he had had a compliant doctor prescribe for him seven days of "balneotherapy." They can't say anything, he explained. He was referring to his employers, I think. He explained that with that term "balneotherapy," you were sitting pretty. Let them send someone to check on me, he said. Then he moved on to politics and asked if Italy could be saved.

Obviously not, if everyone's like the two of us, I said.

He found that very amusing: it must have seemed like the start of a friendship, or something of the sort. He decided we were made for one another, then he left. He had to go home a little early because the next day his neighbors had invited him to eat eggplant: the connection between the two things must have seemed so obvious as to need no explanation.

So I stayed, and I was the last. It's another thing I like: to have a restaurant close around me, at night. To notice that they have begun to switch off the lights, to turn the chairs upside down on the tables. I like it especially when you see the waiters leave to go home, dressed like ordinary people, without the white jacket or the smock, suddenly returned to earth. They walk a little crooked, they seem like forest animals coming out of a spell.

That evening, however, I didn't even see them. The fact is that I was writing. I don't even remember paying the bill, for instance. I was writing in my mind: about when the young Bride left. It had to happen, sooner or later, and the day it happened they all knew to make the most appropriate gestures, suggested by upbringing and proved by decades of decorum. Questions were forbidden. The banality of good wishes was avoided. They didn't like to give in to sentimentality. When they saw her disappear around the bend, no one would have been able to say where she was going: but the biblical delay of the Son, and the suspension of time that that delay had stamped on their days, had left them ill equipped to question the faint relationship that usually holds together a departure and an arrival, an intention and an action. So they watched her leave as, basically, they had seen her arrive: ignorant of everything, aware of everything.

The young Bride went to settle her eighteen years in the place that seemed to her most appropriate and least illogical. The result of such a mental operation may appear surprising now, but it should be remembered that never for an instant, dwelling in the abstract world of the Family, had that girl stopped learning. So now she knew that there are not many destinies but a single story, and that the only exact gesture is repetition. She wondered where she should wait for the Son, sure that he would return, and where the Son would return, sure that she would wait for him forever. She had no doubts about the answer. She appeared at the brothel, in the city, and asked if she could live there.

It's not exactly a job that you can learn in a day, said the Portuguese Woman.

I'm not in a hurry, said the young Bride. I'm waiting for someone.

When she had been earning her living for almost two years in that way, someone sent for her in the middle of the night. She was in a room with a Russian traveler—a man around forty, very nervous and unusually well brought up. The moment she touched him for the first time, the young Bride had understood that he was a homosexual and didn't know it.

In reality they know it perfectly well, the Portuguese

woman had once explained to her. It's that they can't dare to say it to themselves.

And so what do they expect from us? the young Bride had asked.

That we help them lie to themselves.

Then she had reeled off seven tricks to enable them to have pleasure and emerge at peace with themselves.

As the young Bride had later been able to observe repeatedly, the seven tricks were infallible: so she was moving elegantly toward the first when she was summoned. Since the unbreakable rule of the brothel was not to interrupt for any reason in the world the work of the girls, she realized that something special had happened. Yet she didn't think of the Son. Not that she had stopped waiting for him or believing in his return. Rather: if she had had any remaining doubts, she had killed them all the day Comandini appeared at the brothel, without having himself announced. He had asked for her and introduced himself with his hat in his hand. They hadn't seen each other for more than a year.

I would like to speak to you for a moment, he had explained.

The young Bride hated him.

The price is the same, she had said, if you just want to talk it's your business.

So Comandini had paid a not negligible sum to sit with the young Bride, in a room with vaguely Ottoman furnishings, and tell her the truth. Or at least what he knew of the truth. He told her starting from when he had stopped getting news of the Son. He explained the whole business of the deliveries, starting with the two rams. He explained that in fact the Son's last known act had been to buy a small cutter in Newport. He added that there was no news of his possible death, or of any accident that might have happened to him. He had disappeared into nothingness, and that was it.

The young Bride had nodded. Then she had summarized the whole thing in her own way.

Good. Then he's alive and will return.

Then she had asked if she should take off her clothes.

It should unfortunately be noted that Comandini hesitated a long instant before saying No, thank you, getting up, and heading toward the door.

He was leaving when the young Bride stopped him with a question.

Why in the world did you send *Don Quixote*?

I beg your pardon?

Why the hell, with all the books that exist, did you send *Don Quixote*?

Comandini had to bring into focus a memory that evidently he hadn't considered useful to keep within reach. Then he explained that he didn't know much about books, he had just chosen a title he happened to see on the cover of a volume left in a corner in the Mother's room.

In the Mother's room? asked the young Bride.

Exactly, answered Comandini, with a certain harshness. Then, without saying goodbye, he left.

And so, as she walked along the corridor, wrapping a light cloak around her chest, the young Bride could have thought of the Son—she would have had reason to do so, and even desire. Yet, ever since an uncle consumed by fever had arrived in place of the man who gave a meaning to her youth, the young Bride had stopped expecting from life predictable moves. And so she merely let herself be led—her mind unburdened by thoughts, her heart absent—to the room where someone was waiting for her.

She went in and saw Modesto and the Father.

They were both dressed with flawless elegance. The Father was lying on the bed, the features of his face contorted.

Modesto gave two small coughs. The young Bride had

never heard them before, but she understood perfectly. She read in them a studied mixture of dismay, surprise, embarrassment, and nostalgia.

Yes, she said, with a smile.

Grateful, Modesto bowed and moved away from the bed, taking the first steps backward and then turning around as if a gust of wind, and not an inconvenient choice, had decided for him. He left the room, and this book, without saying a word.

Then the young Bride approached the Father. They looked at each other. He was extremely pale, and his chest was jerking uncontrollably. He breathed as if he were biting the air, he couldn't control his eyes. He seemed to have aged a thousand years. He gathered all the energy he still had available and uttered, with a great struggle and unsuspected firmness, a single sentence.

I will not die at night, I will die in the light of the sun.

Instinctively, the young Bride understood everything and looked up at the window. Only darkness filtered through the half-closed blinds. She turned to check the time on the clock that in that room, as in all the others, measured, with a certain indulgence, the time for the work. She didn't know when dawn would break. But she understood that they had several hours now to vanquish and a destiny to dissolve. She decided that they would make it.

Very quickly she reviewed the possible actions she could take. She chose one that had the flaw of being risky and the value of being inevitable. She left the room, went back along the corridor, entered the room where the girls kept their things, opened the drawer that was hers, took out a small object—a gift that was immensely precious to her—and, clutching it in her hand, returned to the Father. She locked the door of the room, approached the bed, and took off her cloak. She went back in her mind to a precise image, of the Mother holding between her legs the Father of the Father, so many years earlier, stroking his hair and speaking to him in a whisper, as if he were alive. Since she had learned that the only exact act is repetition, she climbed onto the bed, drew near the Father, lifted his body, and very gently placed it between her legs and on her chest. She was certain that he knew what she was doing.

She waited for the Father's breath to become a little more regular, and took the gift that was so precious to her. It was a small book. She showed it to the Father and read the title, in a whisper.

How to Abandon Ship.

The Father smiled, because he didn't have the strength to laugh and because those who have a sense of humor have it forever.

The young Bride opened the book to the first page and began to read aloud. Since she had leafed through it many times, she knew that it was identical to the Father: meticulous, rational, slow, irrefutable, apparently detached, secretly poetic. She tried to read as well as she could, and when she felt the Father's body acquire weight, or lose will, she accelerated the rhythm, to chase away death. It was on page 47, more or less in the middle of the chapter devoted to the rules of politeness that are imposed on board a lifeboat, when through the slats of the blinds a light just veined with orange began to filter. The young Bride saw it skimming the cream-colored pages, on every letter and in its own voice. She didn't stop reading, but she realized that any weariness in her had vanished. She continued rolling out the surprisingly numerous reasons that advise settling women and children in the prow, and only when she moved on to examine the pros and cons of rubber life jackets did she see the Father turn his face toward the window, and remain with his eyes wide open, in the light, stunned. Then she read a few more words, more slowly, and then some words in a whisper—and then silence. The Father kept staring at the light. He blinked his eyelids, at a certain point, to chase away the tears that he hadn't taken into account. He sought the young Bride's hand and squeezed it. He said something. The young Bride didn't understand and then she leaned over the Father to hear better. He repeated:

Tell my son that the night is over.

He died just as the sun rose above the horizon, and there was no death rattle, no movement, only a breath like so many others, the last.

The young Bride looked for a heartbeat, in the body she was holding in her arms, and didn't find it. So she ran the palm of her hand over the Father's face to close his eyes, in a gesture that has forever been the privilege of the living. Then she opened the small book with the blue cover again, and continued reading. She had no doubt that the Father would have liked that, and in some passages she felt that no funeral oration could have been more apt. She didn't stop until the end, and, reaching the last sentence, she read it very slowly, as if to protect herself from the risk of its breaking.

Four years later—as I happened to write days ago, in my mind, while I was staring, without seeing it, at a sea that I will nevermore abandon—a man with an anomalous fascination appeared at the brothel; his simple clothes were elegant and he possessed a strong, unnatural calm. He crossed the salon almost without looking around, and stopped confidently in front of the young Bride, who, sitting on a chaise longue, a champagne flute in her hand, was listening with amusement to the confessions of a retired minister.

Seeing him, the young Bride narrowed her eyes slightly. Then she got up.

She stared at the man's face, the lean features, the long hair pulled back, the beard that framed his lips, slightly parted.

You, she said.

The Son took the champagne flute away from her and

offered it to the retired minister, without a word. Then he took the young Bride by the hand and led her away with him.

Emerging into the street, they stopped a moment, to breathe the sparkling air of evening. All of life lay ahead.

The Son took off his jacket, which was of a rough wool and an enchanting color, and placed it over the young Bride's shoulders. Then, without the slightest hint of rebuke, and in an almost childlike tone of curiosity, he asked her a question.

Why in a brothel?

The young Bride knew the answer with absolute precision, but she kept it to herself.

Here I ask the questions, she said.